FORBIDDEN

LIPSTICK CONFESSIONS SERIES

FORBIDDEN

CLAIRE WRIGHT
WITH
G.P. TAYLOR

Authentic

18 17 16 15 14 13 12   7 6 5 4 3 2 1

First published in 2012 by Authentic Media Limited
52 Presley Way, Crownhill, Milton Keynes, MK8 0ES
www.authenticmedia.co.uk

British Library Cataloguing in Publication Data

A catalogue record for this book is available from the
British Library

ISBN: 978-1-85078-900-0

Cover Design by David Smart
Printed and bound by CPI Group (UK) Ltd., Croydon, CR0 4YY

Chapter One

'David? David!'

The man stared at himself in the mirror, bracing himself against the basin with both hands. The clasps of his cufflinks dug painfully into his wrists, and his jacket was too tight. He shook his head irritably. The chairman of a multinational oil company skulking in a bathroom? It wouldn't do. There was a sharp knock on the door.

'David, come on. They're waiting.'

'Just give me a second.'

Concentrating on his facial muscles, he forced his face to adopt a relaxed, peaceful expression. It was nowhere near happy, but it would do. What would they all expect anyway? A second knock on the door.

'You can do this.'

David sighed. Of course he could do it. He gave speeches every day of his life. Besides, he thought wryly, drying his hands on the scratchy towel by the basin, what choice did he have? Half the crowd was Italian and hardly known for their reserve. If he didn't go out there they'd charge the toilet, drag him out and consider it all part of the entertainment. He'd never known such a bunch of jokers. David screwed his eyes shut as thoughts of his wife's frequent practical jokes flashed into his mind. The year she'd sewn his trouser legs up on April Fool's day, and howled to see him stumbling about the bedroom, unable to find his feet; the exploding pen she used to hand him when he least expected it; even the old breakfast trick with an empty eggshell upside down in its eggcup. Time and time again he fell for them, and she never tired of the tricks. David shook his head, trying to clear the residual melancholy from his brain. That way lies danger, he reminded himself. There was no point in delaying any further.

'Right.' He threw the door open, causing the tall, thin man outside to jump violently. 'Come on, Nathan,' David said, striding out of the shaded porch at the entrance of the church onto the sleepy village street. 'Let's do this.'

Nathan straightened up to his full height, towering a whole head above David, and clapped his old friend on the shoulder. 'Right you are,' he said, bracingly. They crossed the road, heading for an enormous marquee in the field beyond. 'The worst part's over now,' Nathan offered by way of encouragement. David kept his eyes on the delicately draped entrance to the marquee, through which the throng of guests was visible, humming and buzzing like bees in a hive.

'You think so?'

'Certainly.' David didn't believe him, but he appreciated the vote of confidence. The friends passed through the wooden barred gate, garlanded with primrose-coloured ribbons for the occasion. David's feet felt leaden, dragging over the freshly mown grass. *I can't do this*, he thought desperately, panic increasing with every step. *I need my wife*. His back itched, the morning suit weighing so heavily on him that even the expensive cotton shirt irritated his skin in the June heat, and he wished that his daughter, Sofia, had not insisted on the top hat. No matter what he did, it refused to stay put on his head. If he crammed it on with any degree of force the damned thing exacted revenge by trying to scalp him when he removed it, leaving large tufts of his hair standing upright at most unnatural angles. Nathan gave him a surreptitious nudge.

'Here come the heavies.'

'What? Oh, no,' groaned David. A small Italian woman had emerged from the marquee and was bearing down on them with unmistakeable purpose, a fringed violet flapper dress swishing about her knees as she ran. Proportioned with roughly equal height and width, she ought to have looked ridiculous. To David she appeared as she always did to him, with the authority of a Roman general, her grey hair streaming behind her like the plume of an officer's helmet. Was it the Latin blood, he wondered, or that intangible gene common to mothers-in-law the world over?

'Save me, Nathan.'

'No chance.'

'Please!'

'I'm a senior advisor in Globe Oil, not your bodyguard.'

'You're off duty and you're my oldest living friend.'

'The answer is still no,' Nathan grinned, falling back a little as the old woman beckoned furiously at them. 'Besides,' he said, mildly, 'my Italian is rusty. I'd only cause offence.'

'Thanks a lot,' growled David.

'Hey, any time.'

David raised his hands towards his mother-in-law in a gesture that managed to combine both apology and surrender. 'Sorry, Maria.'

'Hurry!' she hissed, taking his arm and dragging him towards the marquee. 'They are all waiting.'

'Sorry,' he repeated, marvelling at her uncanny knack of putting him on the back foot. Here he was, arguably one of the most articulate men in the UK oil business, and all he could do was mumble like a surly teenager. How did she do it? Maria glared up at him, her bright eyes piercing his discomfort like a hot needle. 'Where have you been?' she demanded.

'I, er . . . er . . .' David fought for composure, acutely aware of Nathan beside him, silent amusement rolling off him in waves.

'Call of nature,' Nathan put in.

'There are perfectly good toilets behind the marquee,' she snapped.

'Yes, but they're . . . you know . . .' Nathan wrinkled his nose. 'Portaloos. The church has a proper toilet.'

'I sent you to fetch him back,' she accused.

'I did!'

Maria rolled her eyes at him and turned away. 'And you!' She smacked David on the arm as though rebuking a naughty child. 'Why so fussy? You English and your toilet habits. I will never understand.' She halted abruptly at the entrance to the marquee and looked them up and down. 'So,' she sniffed. David realized he was feeding his top hat through his hands in anxious circles and forced himself to stop. Maria jerked her head towards the marquee. 'Inside. We are running behind. The staff are waiting to serve the cake.' With that, she strode off.

David glanced at Nathan. 'Shut up.'

'I didn't say a word.'

'Shut up anyway.'

He squared his shoulders, took a long, slow breath, and followed her in.

As a general rule, Nathan disliked the use of marquees as venues for wedding receptions. True, his opinion was grossly skewed by memories of his own wedding reception, much of which had been spent huddling around the braziers for warmth while the guests queued repeatedly for the chance to stand near the hog roasting spit in the hope of thawing their fingers out. One of the first post-university weddings all those years ago, the disastrous shoestring budget reception had become the stuff of legend among their friends. He and his wife, Jenny, laughed about it now, but Nathan had retained an abiding hatred of marquees ever since. However, he reminded himself, theirs had been a winter wedding. June was far more suitable and today's guests could have no complaints about the venue. Young Sofia had worked wonders with the décor here, swathing the covered cream chairs with chiffon swags in primrose yellow and cornflower blue. Large circular bowls of floating candles in the centre of each table added subtle ambience, while simple miniature vases of mixed wild flowers positioned by every lady's place setting doubled as table decorations and charming favours. Tasteful without being the least bit flashy, Nathan thought, making his way unobtrusively round the edge of the marquee and sliding back into his seat. More importantly, nobody was liable to get frostbite as the evening progressed. Stuck at home with their three small children, Jenny would be eagerly waiting to hear all about the day, down to the tiniest detail. Nathan dutifully did his best to take it all in for her benefit.

Table six was a good spot, close enough to the action but far enough from the top table to be safe from Maria's merciless gaze. A stocky man with a thatch of sandy hair reached across the table with a bottle of red wine as Nathan took his place. 'Top-up?'

'Never more needed,' said Nathan gratefully, pushing his empty glass forward. The man lowered his voice and leaned in as he poured. 'Alright, is he?'

Nathan kept his face neutral. 'Oh, yes,' he said with the bland smile normally reserved for the press and colleagues he mistrusted. Being neither of these, the man looked hurt.

'Come off it, Nathan. It's me asking, not some journo hack.' Richard Hampton, a geology geek and until a few years ago a die-hard field development explorer and petroleum engineer, off hunting for new resources of crude oil, had known David and Nathan for over twenty years. A couple of years ago David had headhunted him for the post of Vice-President of Technical Services, and Rich had reluctantly shelved his geology books and accepted the inevitability of a desk job.

'Sorry, Rich. Force of habit.' The art of dissembling and deflecting questions had become so ingrained in Nathan during his own scramble up the career ladder it was difficult to switch off, even in the most trusted company. Nathan took a deep gulp of wine and sat back, scanning the faces round the table. Company didn't get much more trusted than this, the old Oxford crowd. He realized Rich was still watching him patiently, waiting for a real reply. 'What can I say, mate?' he sighed, one bony shoulder lifting in a characteristic half-shrug. 'He's holding it together, but – well. You know the score.' Rich nodded sadly, his eyes suddenly down-cast.

'Yeah,' he said, softly. 'I know it. I can't believe it's been two years.' He had loved David's wife like a sister. They all had. Nathan sighed. Bright, beautiful Carlotta had left a hole in many hearts, including his. Seeing his friend fighting tears, he swiftly changed the subject. Rich didn't do public emotion.

'How's Beth?' he asked, knowing that talk of Rich's new wife was guaranteed to swing the conversation into a brighter sphere. 'What a shame she couldn't make it.'

Rich's face brightened instantly. 'She's great,' he replied. 'She really wanted to be here, but she had a shoot. Tried to get out of it, but the agency insisted on her.' His voice radiated the pride he felt in his wife's achievements. By all accounts, his pride was not misplaced, Nathan reflected. At 35, Beth was one of the most sought-after photographers in the magazine industry, having abandoned early modelling opportunities for a career behind the lens. That was no small accomplishment.

'Has she met David yet?' he asked casually, though he knew the answer.

Rich shook his head. 'We can never get a date when everyone's free. He missed the wedding, of course, and now either I'm away, or Beth's off on location, and David's schedule is –'

'Insane?' Nathan suggested.

Rich laughed. 'I certainly wouldn't like to be in charge of his diary,' he agreed. 'It appears to be a locked room with no windows.'

'Email him,' Nathan advised. 'Jog his memory. They'd get on well.' Privately, he knew that David had deliberately avoided a meeting with Rich and his wife. Not through bitterness, certainly. David was a man of enormous heart. He had been genuinely delighted that Rich had found someone after his long years as a bachelor. It was just that Carlotta's death had delivered such a crippling blow that he was still patching himself up, and probably would be for years to come. Nathan's opinion was that David feared to see a reflection of his own former happiness, lest the joy of others burst open the shoddy stitches of his own wounds. It was self-preservation, nothing more. That, Nathan knew, was why today was so hard for David. What could be closer to home than his own daughter's wedding, the guest list peppered with Carlotta's family and friends? It was testing his composure to the limit. Looking over to the top table, Nathan's mouth went dry as he saw David stand and tap his glass for silence. Nathan offered up a fervent prayer that his friend's great charisma would carry him through.

David looked slowly around the marquee, trying to meet the eye of a couple of guests on each table while the noise in the room gradually ebbed away. It was an old trick he'd been taught years ago by one of his English teachers. He couldn't recall the man's name, but a vivid mental image of him had stayed with David: a short, volatile man in a tweed suit, his thick, bushy eyebrows pulled into a frown of concentration as he sought to extract a passable poetry recital from David. Kipling or Yeats, David didn't remember which. 'Always take your time, boy,' he'd insisted, jabbing a nicotine-stained finger into David's chest when he stumbled over the opening line. 'Don't fear the silence. Use it, understand?'

'No, sir.' Exasperated, the man had gripped the young David by the shoulder and propelled him to the window, gesturing at the school grounds below them.

'Do you skim stones on the lake?' he'd demanded. David had eyed him nervously as the class tittered. Skimming stones was against school rules. 'Answer me!'

'Yes, sir.'

'Good. And are stones best skimmed on calm or choppy water?'

'Calm water, sir.'

'Good. Now, then. Think of these . . .' His arm swept out in a gesture that took in the entire class, '. . . as your lake. Words are your stones.' The teacher had stared hard at David. 'Concentrate, boy. If ever you have to speak in public, and I certainly can't imagine you will,' – more laughter from the class – 'But!' he barked. 'If you do, then remember to wait. Wait for the lake to be completely still before you let those stones fly.' David had gulped and nodded, wanting only to get through the required four stanzas and fade back in among his classmates. The teacher's fingers had dug hard into his shoulder, making his eyes water from the pain.

'Remember that, boy,' he'd insisted. 'Remember it. Some day you might thank me.'

Many times since that day, David had. It was arguably the most useful piece of advice he had ever been given, certainly in terms of furthering his career. When the silence was absolute, he waited a moment longer, smiled down at his beautiful daughter, and began to speak.

The bride and groom left at 11 o'clock to wild cheers and the traditional clattering of tin cans fixed to the back of their car. At midnight the party was still in full swing. After several hours of intermittent shuffling on the fringes of the dance floor while the younger contingent of guests strutted their stuff with admirable abandon, Nathan conceded defeat. He'd rather be tucked up at home with Jenny and a single malt. I won't be old until I switch from whisky to Ovaltine, he told himself, glancing at his watch. Midnight was a respectable time to leave. After a swift circuit of the marquee to say his goodbyes, Nathan retrieved his jacket and stepped out into the dark. It was a beautiful, cloudless night, the constellations sharp and clear overhead. Nathan craned his neck to look up at them, a feeling of peace settling over him. Perhaps Carlotta was watching him from somewhere up there, he mused. It was a comforting thought.

'Nathan?' He turned as Rich popped out of the marquee. 'I can't find David,' he said, his face flushed with concern. 'Are you taking him home?'

'Yeah, it's OK,' Nathan replied. 'I know where he is.'

'Right.' Rich waited a moment but Nathan didn't elaborate. 'So, I'll see you soon, I hope?' he said awkwardly, stepping forward to grasp Nathan's hand.

'Count on it,' said Nathan, returning the handshake firmly. 'I'll be in touch. Take care.' He set off across the field, keeping his stride long and unhurried in case his friend was still watching. In actual fact, he didn't know where David was. He might have seen Nathan on the dance floor and called a taxi, or taken up one of the offers of accommodation from old friends in the village. He could have slipped off to the local pub for a quiet drink and the chance to process the day's events in peace, though the chances of him going unrecognized there were virtually nonexistent. In theory, there were any number of places David could be. In reality, only one place in this village, on this night, made sense. Nathan knew where to look.

With a quick glance over his shoulder, he left the field and crossed the road to the church where the marriage had been celebrated that afternoon. Quietly opening the gate to the churchyard, Nathan trod grubby remnants of confetti into the gravelled path as he made his way silently to the small plot of graves where Carlotta lay. Married and buried here, and now her daughter married here in her turn. There was symmetry to it all, but as the kneeling figure came into view, its forehead pressed to the cold headstone in a gesture so heartbreakingly bereft, Nathan saw tremendous cruelty in Sofia's choice. Unintended, but inexcusable nonetheless. He stopped, reluctant to intrude on a grief that was still fiercely private, but unwilling to leave his friend to suffer alone. Long moments passed before David sensed his presence. Then he sat back on his heels, his head bowed, waiting for the familiar pressure of the hand on his shoulder. When it came, he turned his face up to meet Nathan's steady gaze. No words were spoken to fill the silence. Sometimes even the best stones wouldn't skim on a lake, however skilfully thrown. Instead, Nathan pulled David to his feet and set an arm about his shoulders. Together, they turned for home.

Chapter Two

It was past 1 o'clock when Nathan manoeuvred his car into the drive, killing the engine quickly to avoid waking the children. Paradoxically, the absence of the diesel engine's throaty hum caused David to wake. He sat up, momentarily disorientated by the silence and the darkness. The drive had given him time to collect himself, but he looked utterly spent, the cost of his efforts clearly printed on his face. David had a natural boyishness about him, somehow retaining a fresh, young aura as the years rolled by. Tonight, his brown eyes appeared even darker than usual, shadowed and heavy-lidded with fatigue. Beneath the thick, black head of hair that he was secretly so proud of, deep lines were apparent on his forehead. Nathan had never noticed them before. It was as if David's long-held grief, once loosed, had extended its claws and scratched them into place that very night. Eyeing his friend in the gloom, Nathan wondered whether David had managed to safely trap it once more or whether it was now an uncontainable monster bent on wreaking havoc in his life. In all their lives, he thought, a prescient shudder running down his spine.

'What?' David asked.

'Nothing,' said Nathan softly, unbuckling his seatbelt. 'Come on. Spare room's all ready for you.'

'There was no need, Nathan,' David began, his words still slurred from sleep.

'It's done,' said Nathan. 'Besides,' he added with a yawn, 'You'll get a better breakfast this way.'

He got out of the car to quell any further protests and took a deep, slow breath, enjoying the flower-scented air that he always claimed was particular to his garden. Home Air, he called it. The roses were doing remarkably well this year, and the magnolia tree had hung on well past its normal season. All down to Jenny, of course, he thought, feeling the familiar twang of envy. Gardening stood high on the list of pleasures that Nathan had sacrificed since he'd been promoted to the lofty heights of director and senior advisor for Europe as part of the Globe Oil group. David climbed out of the car and stood beside him, letting the companionable silence flow soothingly around him. He felt bruised all over, as though someone had peeled off his skin and stuck it back on inside out with all the nerve endings exposed. Even the light touch of Nathan's hand on his shoulder made him wince. He shook his head at Nathan's concerned expression and forced a smile.

'It's nothing. I was miles away, that's all.'

Shrugging their shoes off on the doorstep, they entered the house like ghosts, shadowing each other's steps on the staircase before peeling off in opposite directions on the upper landing with a silent, signed goodnight. At the door to his room Nathan paused, remembering his whisky, safely barricaded among the crystalware in the glass-fronted kitchen cabinet, well out of reach of little hands. Two-year-old Michael had lately taken to mountaineering exploits with a degree of success that provoked a mixture of fear and admiration in his parents. Nathan cocked his head in the direction of the spare room, listening for sounds of life. Perhaps he should bring up a couple of glasses, offer one to David? A muffled thud came from the guest room, sounding very like a fully clothed man hitting the bed. Nathan grinned and opened his own door a crack to see if Jenny was still awake and in need of a nightcap. His grin widened at the sight of the whisky decanter and crystal glass placed ready on the bedside table by his thoughtful wife.

'Oh, I love you,' he said fervently, collapsing onto the bed where his wife lay reading.

'Ow!' Jenny drew her legs up sharply beneath the duvet, almost knocking over the gin and tonic balanced on her chest. She swiftly transferred the glass to the floor, out of harm's way, and levered herself upright. 'Are you drunk?' she demanded, tucking her long, mousy hair behind her ears.

'No!' protested Nathan, looking wounded. 'I tell you I love you all the time, not just when I'm drunk.'

Jenny rolled her eyes. 'Yes, but you don't usually fall over when you say it. You'll be saying I'm beautiful next. Don't!' she said as he opened his mouth. 'Now get off,' she said affectionately, reaching across to slap him on the leg. 'You're messing up the duvet.' Nathan peered at his trousers and saw a thick hem of dried mud on each leg.

'Damn country weddings,' he grumbled, rolling aside and brushing the bits off the bed as best he could. 'Why couldn't Sofia have got married in town like civilized people?'

'Oh, stop moaning, you old party pooper,' his wife replied, cheerfully. 'I spent three hours this afternoon wearing a saucepan on my head and fighting off monsters with nothing but a wooden spoon and a bucket. *And* I found Michael trying to shin up the curtains in the lounge again.'

'How was Abigail? Any dramatic Last Stands today?' At 4, their daughter was prone to remarkable fits of temper. Jenny was a master at defusing potential Armageddon situations but Nathan tended to laugh, which caused instant spontaneous combustion.

'She's been great today,' replied Jenny, her top half-vanishing over the side of the bed as she retrieved her gin and tonic. 'She even helped bath Rory after tea.'

Nathan raised his eyebrows. 'That's a turn-up for the books. Poor old Rory hardly gets a look-in normally.' The baby's arrival five months ago had sparked considerable jealousy from the other children, particularly Abigail. All perfectly normal but still, it saddened Nathan, more so because Rory was a placid, chubby-cheeked delight who slept for England and was by far the least bother of the three. Jenny shrugged.

'Abi just needs time.' She threw the covers back and patted the space beside her. 'Get in,' she commanded, her eyes gleaming at the prospect of a good gossip. 'Enough baby talk. I want to hear all about the wedding. Were the Italian mob there in force? Monster-in-law Maria? Did Rich bring his new wife? What was the dress like?' Busy wrestling his suit off, Nathan pretended not to hear. '*Nathan!*' He grunted in surprise as a pillow thumped into his back.

'Hold your horses, I'm coming.' He kicked his clothes into a pile on the floor and sat down heavily on the bed, stretching over for the whisky bottle. 'I've definitely earned this,' he sighed, pouring a generous measure into the glass.

No ice, but he wasn't about to complain. Jenny wriggled over to him and Nathan gathered her in close, leaning back against the headboard. He planted a kiss on the top of her head, breathing in the familiar scent of her. Talcum powder, baby shampoo, the brand of perfume she'd worn for years, and undertones of something he could never quite identify that was purely her. It was like inhaling peace in vapour form. 'It's good to be home,' he said, swirling his drink with his free hand. Jenny looked up at him, surprised at the evident relief in his voice.

'It was OK, wasn't it?' she asked, her freckled face wrinkling with concern.

'Yes and no,' Nathan answered, sipping from his glass. 'It was a great day, just as Carlotta would have wanted it, I think. Sofia had everything just so.'

'Never mind all that.' Jenny made a chopping motion with the flat of her hand, as though cutting all thoughts of fashion and gossip from her mind. 'How was David? He got through it, didn't he?'

'Publicly, he held it together. Pulled it off brilliantly, in fact, just as you predicted. Privately . . .' Nathan exhaled slowly, letting the tension flow out of him. 'Privately, meaning just the two of us, he went into meltdown.' He felt his wife's body jerk beside him at this pronouncement. David was famously self-controlled in all aspects of his life. Meltdown wasn't a word that anyone, friend or enemy, would associate with him.

'What do you mean? Like, *total* meltdown?'

Nathan nodded. 'He nearly bottled it before the speech. Shut himself in the toilet at the church for quarter of an hour.'

'He didn't!'

'I promise you he did. Not like him, is it?'

'No.' Jenny smoothed her hand over the creases in the duvet, her fingers tracing the appliquéd floral stitching as her mind apparently conjured up the scene. 'Even given the circumstances, that's just . . . not David.'

'There's more.' Nathan drained the glass and set it down on the table by the old reading lamp he'd kept from their college days. 'Later on, I found him at Carlotta's grave. He completely gave way, Jenny. I've never seen him like that, never. He was clinging to the headstone.'

'Oh, no.' Tears welled in her eyes and she dashed them away, suddenly angry. 'I knew they shouldn't have held the wedding there,' she said, bunching the duvet in her fist. 'He's been bottling things up for a long time.' She rounded on Nathan, and he could see that she was furious that their friend had been brought so low. 'What was Sofia *thinking*?' she demanded, jabbing her husband in the chest with an accusing finger. 'She should have had more sense.' Nathan held his hands up, recoiling from her anger. 'Hey, don't shoot the messenger.' He rubbed his chest. 'Your nails are sharp.'

'I'm sorry.' Jenny sat back and folded her arms as if to prevent herself inflicting any further injury. 'I like Sofia, you know that,' she continued quietly, obviously trying to contain her protective instincts towards David. 'It just seems –' Nathan ducked as her arm swept out again, palm up, as though offering the question up to the higher powers of the universe, ' – needlessly cruel.'

'I thought the same. Maybe she just . . . felt close to her mother there. It's not her fault that David is completely shut off from it all, is it?'

Jenny pursed her lips, and Nathan could see her innate sense of fairness warring with the desire to be cross with someone, anyone, about David's hurt. 'I suppose not,' she said, grudgingly.

They sat side by side in silence for a while, each of them contemplating their concerns for David. Though equally valid, their perspectives were radically different. Jenny had long foreseen problems with David's coping mechanism for grief, maintaining that internalizing it would either give him an ulcer or a nervous breakdown of epic proportions; possibly both. More, she felt that his relationship with his daughter was directly suffering from his refusal to discuss Carlotta, or to address the loss directly. For David, Carlotta was dead and he couldn't bring her back. End of. It was too cut and dried, too clinical, she argued. Nathan had banned her from speaking to David about it, fearing their home would no longer be a place of refuge and welcome relief, but be added to David's list of places to avoid. Although Nathan felt his friend's pain keenly, he couldn't help but look at the wider picture. Whenever the topic of David and Carlotta came up between he and Jenny, he found himself staring at the same image over and over again. A house of cards. If David fell, he could bring a hell of a lot tumbling down with him, and when you were the chairman of a powerful company such as Globe Oil, it would be significantly more than a six foot drop. It felt like a warning, if you believed in such things. Jenny found Nathan's view callous, he found hers too blinkered. Not that the individual didn't matter; of course not. But all individual actions had consequences, and it followed that the greater the individual, the greater the consequence.

They'd more or less reached an amicable decision not to discuss it, but the day's events seemed to demand it. Jenny broke the silence first.

'How is he now?'

Nathan sighed. 'I don't know, darling,' he admitted, his eyes sweeping the room as though the answer could be found amid the old oak chests and wardrobes, the piles of neatly folded washing, or the abandoned toys scattered like a treasure trail across the floor. 'Calm. Tired. Exhausted, I think.'

'Is he going to be OK?'

'He's David. He *makes* things be OK.'

'Even when they're not.'

'Especially when they're not. You know that as well as I do, love.' They wrapped their arms around each other and lay down. 'You won't see a trace of it in him tomorrow,' Nathan predicted, reaching out to snap the light off. 'He'll be quite himself again, you'll see.'

'Or appear to be,' Jenny retorted, her voice muffled against his chest. They said no more, both recognizing the old circular debate. But then, in the last moments before sleep took them, Nathan heard his wife ask, 'Who's going to make things OK for him?'

At the other end of the landing, David was asking the same question, over and over again, throwing it out into the darkness. But night was a time for questions and the silence tossed it back, offering no answers in return for his persistence, only more questions, piling one upon the other on his chest until he was struggling to breathe. He thought the weight of them would crush him. Part of him wanted it to, but it was no use. Even as the thought took shape in his mind it was knocked out by a roundhouse punch. Though his sparring days were long gone, the fighter in David would never give in.

David woke early. Too early. The thin floral curtains did a poor job of shielding him from the light and were no defence at all against the insistent chirping of the local dawn chorus. They were making such a racket it felt as though there was a whole bird's nest tucked under his pillow. David rolled over and groaned, stiff and uncomfortable from sleeping in his clothes. 'Urgh.' His throat felt rough, and his tongue was so swollen it was like a foreign object in his mouth. The last thing he needed was to be ill, he thought, closing his eyes and willing it away. He rolled off the bed and opened the door of the little wardrobe at the foot of it, selecting a shirt and pair of trousers at random. He and Nathan were roughly the same size, apart from the leg length. It would do until he got home, anyway. Even the chairman of Globe Oil didn't have to wear a suit on Sunday. The previous incumbent had been such a stuffed shirt that his own staff joked that he slept in a three-piece with his top button firmly fastened. It wasn't David's style. Looping the clothes over his arm, he made his way to the bathroom and took a quick shower, closing his eyes against the spray and visualizing all his troubles disappearing down the plughole. It had become like a daily ritual since Carlotta's death. He never opened his eyes, half-fearing that if he did, he would see them running off him in grimy rivulets. It was a stupid little thing but it made him feel better and it had become

. . . habit. But it *definitely* didn't make him weird. Or weak. David was very clear with himself on this point. Everybody had their quirks, didn't they?

Down in the kitchen, David stood gazing out into the garden, cupping a brightly coloured bowl in one hand as he crunched moodily through some over-sugared cereal, the kind that rotted your teeth but came with cool free toys by way of compensation. He was surprised Jenny allowed it in the house, come to think of it. She would be annoyed with him, he thought, watching a squirrel mount an attack on the bird feeder, scaling the post in furtive silence while three finches squabbled overhead, completely oblivious. Jenny always made a point of trying to feed him up with her legendary cooked breakfasts, though no one in their right mind could accuse him of wasting away. 'Chance would be a fine thing,' he muttered, prodding his stomach with the blunt end of his spoon. David glanced back out of the window and saw the squirrel was in position, ready to pounce. He frowned. One against three, but with the element of surprise and the size difference, it was hardly a fair fight. He reached out and banged his fist on the glass as hard as he could. The effect was louder than he expected. Instantly the birds scattered, leaving the squirrel to claim the spoils. 'Shouldn't have interfered.' David shook his head and turned away in disgust. 'Aargh!' He jumped and clutched the bowl instinctively to his chest, spilling soggy cereal down his shirt. Abigail, who had entered the room and come right up behind him without making a sound, removed her thumb from her mouth and eyed him darkly.

'It's Sunday,' she announced, threateningly.

'I know,' he replied, dumping the bowl in the sink and dabbing frantically at the shirt with a dishcloth. 'How are you, Abi?'

'It's Sunday,' she repeated, with the kind of exaggerated patience one normally used for small children and the senile. She thrust her hands into the pockets of her purple butterfly-print pyjamas, her little jaw jutting out aggressively.

'I know it's Sunday.' David rubbed at his unshaven jaw, looking down at the child with wary amusement. The short, auburn bob with its blunt fringe gave her a rather severe look, he felt, but it was the eyes that always got him. Blue like her mother's but brighter, always sparkling with a diamond-hard determination. Facing his goddaughter was like going head to head with Churchill reincarnated. Never give in, never surrender. And always, *always* an agenda. David squatted down to Abigail's level, being careful not to make any sudden moves.

'Are you thinking I should be in church?' he asked, trying to feel his way into the potential conflict zone. 'Because we talked about that, do you remember?'

Withering silence from the enemy camp.

'OK. Do I have to guess? Like a game?'

Silence.

David kept his face straight with great effort, remembering the misunderstanding that had led Abigail to shun him for nearly a whole year. During a huge sustainable energy campaign to raise Globe Oil's profile as an environmentally aware company, the British PR team had come up with the slogan 'For the greater good'. Nathan hadn't realized how much he'd been using the phrase until Abigail had appeared at his bedside one night when he returned from work exceptionally late.

'Daddy, where have you been?'

'At work, darling.'

'Doing things for the Greater God?'

'That's right.'

'Well, in prayers at school today I asked him to let you be back for bathtime,' she said, blue eyes boring accusingly into him. 'And you weren't. I'm not his friend any more.' She had jammed her thumb into her mouth with damning finality, then removed it to add, 'Or yours,' before stomping back to bed, pink pyjamas bristling with righteous indignation. Further discussion the following day had revealed that Abigail thought David was God, since Nathan worked for him. The problem was compounded when Abigail didn't receive a pony for her birthday, having lobbied both God and her parents for several months. This led to a kind of spiritual Cold War and she refused point-blank to speak to David, despite many long and patient explanations on Nathan's part. Even now, they had only progressed to an uneasy truce. Smiling brightly, David cleared his throat and made a show of thinking hard.

'Er . . . it's Sunday, so . . . you get to watch cartoons? No? You get a special breakfast? Something extra fun happens? It's roast chicken dinner day?'

Abigail considered him for a moment, then moved in for the kill, the tip of her freckled nose pushed right up to his. David was backed up against a cupboard door with nowhere to go. 'It's Sunday,' she said in a stage whisper. 'You can't do a big bang.'

'Ah. Right, I see.' His mind worked feverishly. Surely she wasn't old enough to grasp the Creationist theory? Something in his face must have betrayed his total lack of comprehension because Abigail almost head-butted him in frustration.

'Uncle David!' she yelled. 'It's *Mummy's lie-in!*'

'Abigail!' They turned in unison to find Jenny standing in the doorway with her hands on her hips, her hair dishevelled from sleep. Michael's face peeped round the edge of her dressinggown, enjoying the show from a safe distance. Jenny shook her head sternly at Abigail. 'It's Sunday, Abi,' she said.

'I KNOW!' bawled Abigail, the air around her pulsating with rage. '*Tell* him, Mummy!' She kicked the cupboard door, howled with pain and fled the room in floods of tears. Jenny walked calmly to the cooker and plucked a frying-pan from its hanging place on the wall. 'Are you getting up?' she enquired, raising an eyebrow at David, who realized he was still squatting against the kitchen units.

'Uh, yeah.' He stood up, sheepishly brushing gobbets of cereal from Nathan's shirt, not quite sure where to put himself. Jenny shot him an amused look.

'What? I didn't mean to wind her up.'

'Oh, I know, I know. I was just thinking,' she remarked, managing to pour oil into the pan, light the gas and shunt Michael to a safe distance from the hob more or less simultaneously. 'You should let Nathan bring Abigail along to a board meeting. She'd make mincemeat of the directors.'

David chuckled. 'I certainly wouldn't bet against her.'

'Get the bacon out for me, will you?'

'Sure.'

Jenny nodded at her son. 'Go and wake Daddy, Michael. Tell him it's breakfast time.' The little boy scampered off, delighted with his mission. 'Why don't you stay for the day?' Jenny said casually, as David leaned round her to lay a few rashers into the sizzling pan. Too casually.

'No thanks,' he said, quickly. 'I've got a mountain of stuff to get through today. Just a quick breakfast and I'll be off.'

Jenny pointed her wooden spoon at him. 'All work and no play . . .' she tutted.

David shrugged mournfully. 'I know,' he sighed. 'But I was always a dull boy.' He ducked as she threw the spoon at him, and burst out laughing despite himself. Nathan's place was as much home to him as anywhere else these days, but without Carlotta home was just a word for a place like any other. No, he corrected himself. Not like any other. It was worse than that. The presence of people and things only made the empty spaces of her absence bigger, pockets of it everywhere and a constant void at his left hand, where she no longer stood. Work was the only safe place to be.

Chapter Three

Beth was excited. It was her turn to host the bi-monthly committee meeting of Nightingale, the Third-World charity that she volunteered for, and tonight was the night. As dull as it sounded, the work they supported made it all worth it. Founded by a group of artists and musicians, the charity ran small centres in northern Uganda which welcomed children who were victims or witnesses to violence or abuse during the twenty-year humanitarian crisis which ended in 2005, when the government pushed Joseph Kony and the long-feared Lord's Resistance Army out of the country. Ostensibly run as a small school, the staff focused on art therapy and music to support recovery. In recent years, outreach support extending to the returning 1.8 million displaced families had also been added.

Beth travelled out there for a few days once a year, and took all the publicity shots for the charity. On her last trip she'd seen the whole school assembled for choir practice at the beginning and end of each day, their voices soaring in the distinctive close harmonies of African music. Even thinking about it raised the hairs on the back of Beth's neck. Busy as she was with her freelance projects, Beth found herself wanting to give more to the work. Rich worked long hours and could be away for months at a time with foreign postings. The volunteering filled the gap. She had been working on ideas for a new project, and she was hoping for a favourable response when she presented it this evening. Her stomach twitched with butterflies as she ran through the plans in her mind, only half-aware of the meal she was dishing up for her husband. In the nicest possible way, she needed to get him fed and safely out of the way before everyone arrived.

'Rich! Dinner's ready!' she called, ladling generous portions of pasta onto two plates, and carrying them to the kitchen table. She eyed her creation critically, then delved into the fridge and shoved a couple of handfuls of rocket on the edge as an afterthought. It promptly swooned over the side, bitter leaves spilling onto the wooden table. Beth didn't bother scooping it up. The table had been her grandmother's and bore the loving scars of many years of wear and tear, but it was clean. Clean enough, anyway. Beth ran her palm over the pitted surface, knowing every dent and scratch by heart. It was like a fingerprint of her childhood, here the scorch mark where she and her sister had put a hot pan the day they experimented with toffee, there the grooves made by her grandfather carelessly chopping without a board. It was a habit he always apologized for but never gave up, like his cigars. At 4:30 on the dot on baking day he would tramp in from his precious shed, scoop the girls up from their places on the bench beside her grandmother and say, 'Have you made me some goodies today, or must I eat you instead?' in his big, booming voice. Sticky-fingered and covered in flour, Beth and Cerys would hide their faces in his neck and shriek out the names of their offering. 'Jam tarts! Lemon drizzle! Gingerbread!' while their grandmother watched fondly and pretended to scold her husband for 'getting the children all whipped up'. Saturdays at her grandparents' were the best, thought Beth. Delighted as they were with her success, the old couple were nearly ill with pride when Cerys went on to catering college and opened a trendy bakery in Brighton, all thanks to those early years at the kitchen table.

'Earth to Beth?'

'Hmm?' She jumped and saw her husband in the doorway, laughing at her dreamy expression. 'Sorry,' she said, hastily pulling out one of the old chairs and sitting down. 'I was miles away.' She tucked her carefully straightened hair behind her ears and poured them each a glass of water from the carafe in the centre of the table, emptying the remainder into the ceramic vase centrepiece filled with pink roses. They were past their best but hanging on in there, and Beth could never throw a bunch of flowers out until they were well and truly dead. She kept on watering them and trying to jolly them along until the last petal had withered, just in case.

'You looked as though you were trying to commune with the spirits of dead kitchen tables,' Rich grinned, taking his place opposite her.

'Idiot. I was just thinking.'

'Uh-oh. Dangerous business.' He picked up his fork and gave the heaped-up pasta an experimental prod. 'Looks interesting.'

She kicked him under the table. 'It's perfectly edible.'

'I never said it wasn't!'

'Mmph. You implied it.'

'That's simply not true.' Rich scooped up an enormous forkful and pushed it into his mouth. 'See?' he mumbled, pesto sauce dribbling down his chin. 'I love your cooking.' Beth rolled her eyes at him, and tucked into her own meal.

It was impossible to be cross with a man who not only swore undying love on a daily basis, but was willing to eat her 'concoctions' with a smile on his face. Undercooked vegetables? He liked them crunchy. Soggy Yorkshire puddings? Much better than dry ones. Lumpy gravy? Far more filling than the runny stuff. Rich was the kind of person who could find something good to say about pretty much anything. Who wouldn't love a man like that? Not that he was perfect. He made a point of being late whenever possible and left his dirty clothes in mouldering heaps around the house, half-tidied into secret stashes behind bedroom doors, under furniture, in the bottom of the wardrobe. Then he wore odd socks and mismatched outfits with cheerful abandon until Beth managed to smell out the missing laundry and restore it to a state of decency.

'Look,' she'd finally said, frogmarching him to the bathroom on the day she'd found a rancid collection of odd socks under the study desk, which had been fermenting for so long they'd virtually achieved independent living status. 'This is the laundry basket. This is where the washing goes. That's the system, right?'

He had smiled at her in his lopsided, easygoing-Rich-way and agreed that, yes, that was indeed the system. Beth had stared at him, completely bewildered. 'So why do you hide it all?' she'd demanded.

'I don't.'

'You *do!*' she'd insisted, yanking the end of her long, blonde ponytail in sheer frustration. 'You're like . . . like . . .

a paranoid squirrel or something. You can't hide your clothes for the winter, Rich, they stink. Please stop it.'

He'd pursed his lips and frowned. 'I'm not sure I can,' he'd said, thoughtfully. 'I don't realize I'm doing it, I think.'

'But you're so tidy at work,' she'd argued. 'You had to be tidy on all those geeky field development expeditions to sniff out oil, right? You didn't have a choice.'

'No,' he'd agreed, his face suddenly clearing. 'Perhaps that's why I do it.'

'What? Ugh!' Beth had realized she was clutching the awful sock-bundle to her chest, and flung it into the basket as though it were a writhing clutch of snakes.

'Yes, I think that's the answer,' Rich had continued, oblivious to the expression of horror on his wife's face as she'd frantically scrubbed her hands on a fluffy towel. 'I do it because I can. Never realized that before.' Stooping, he'd kissed Beth tenderly on the lips and sauntered off. 'You're a genius.' She had remained in the bathroom for some time with her forehead pressed against the cooling mirror tiles on the wall, and counted to 100. How had he got to 42 without anyone purging him of such a dreadful habit? However, in the grand scheme of things, the Squirrel Thing, as they dubbed it, was a small gripe when set against all the positives in their marriage. As Cerys pointed out, it was no weirder than Beth's cooking anomaly – thanks to their grandmother she could bake any cake you named, but had the unfortunate ability to mangle any savoury recipe, however nice the ingredients. After thirty-five years of fruitless efforts, Beth no longer beat herself up about it and the Hamptons used her cakes and puddings to scour the taste of dinner from their mouths. Either that, or Rich cooked. Beth looked up at her husband, still ploughing loyally through the rubbery pasta, and loved him more than ever.

Almost on cue, he looked up and caught her eye. 'Any cake?' he asked desperately, reaching for his glass of water to swill the food down. Beth did a quick mental inventory of their baking supplies.

'Um . . . no cake, but we've got shortbread and chocolate flapjack.'

'The stuff in the blue tin?'

'Yep.'

His face fell. 'I ate those this morning.'

'What, all of them?'

'I got the munchies,' he said, defensively.

'Don't worry.' Beth pushed her chair back and opened the double doors of their Welsh dresser. 'I saved some in here for the meeting, but there's loads.' She pulled out a circular tin with a floral print design trailing over the lid and set it on the table, deftly pulling the plates away and tipping them into the sink to rid themselves of the sight.

'Thank God.'

'Do you want a plate?'

'No point,' he said, his jaws already working furiously on the first flapjack and the second cupped in his hand.

'Pig,' she said, affectionately, circling the table to drop a kiss on his head.

'Needs must,' he sighed, reaching up to squeeze her hand. 'Go on, get ready for your meeting. I'll be out of your hair in a second.'

'There's no rush,' she protested, though her feet were already walking her towards the sitting-room.

He twisted round in his chair as an alarming possibility apparently came to mind. 'Janet's not coming, is she?'

'Er, not sure,' replied Beth, feigning ignorance. 'I think so.' Janet was a headmistress who had taken early retirement to concentrate on her charity work. She adored Beth, and her behaviour towards Rich veered between steely eyed interrogation – 'I hope you're looking after Beth properly, Richard?' and aggressive flirting – 'I insist that you join me for lunch next time you're in town. I must get to know you better.' Rich was terrified of her.

'Make that half a second,' he said, grabbing a third flapjack and spilling oaty crumbs down his front in his haste to be gone.

'You'll be quite safe upstairs,' Beth said mildly, hiding a smile.

'I'm not risking it. I'll go for a run.' Rich grabbed his running shoes from the jumble of footwear by the back door and shoved them on.

'But we'll be a few hours here,' she pointed out, 'and you already ran this morning.'

'The pub, then.'

'Take your phone,' she suggested. 'I'll call you when the coast is clear.'

'Deal. See you later.'

'Yeah, love you.' By the time the door clicked shut she was already halfway up the stairs, her mind on the work ahead.

Sitting in his office in central London, David was trying to get his mind off the work ahead, just for an hour so he could eat dinner. Lunch seemed a long time ago. Judging from the growl in his stomach, he probably hadn't eaten lunch. He couldn't remember. The woman seated opposite him was making it pretty hard to do anything other than keep his mouth closed to block the irritable remarks surging like waves against his clenched teeth. Amanda Webster was an excellent press officer and nobody would question her diligence but surely, *surely* a woman of her calibre had something better to do at 7.30 p.m. on a Friday night than go over a simple brief for some upcoming interviews? She was stunningly good-looking, hardly the type to stay home alone watching reruns of old television sitcoms and sinking a tub or two of overpriced ice cream. Why was she here?

'Sir?'

David jumped. Amanda was looking at him expectantly, silver pen delicately gripped between perfectly painted fingernails, the nib hovering just above the page of her notepad. Damn. 'Er . . . yes? Please go on,' he said, shifting position in his chair to ease the pressure on his lower back. It was her turn to stare.

'If you could tell me how you want me to proceed with this?'

David cleared his throat uncomfortably. 'I'm sorry, I lost focus there for a second,' he admitted. 'Can you go from the top?'

Her eyes widened. 'Right from the top, sir?'

'No, er, just . . . the last bit.'

'I see.'

It was not right, David thought, that a person could make you shrink with nothing more than an expressively arched eyebrow. Somehow Amanda managed to achieve the effect of looking both at you and through you, as though her gaze was pinned on a far-off destination that only she could see. It was unnerving. Amanda Webster was not like other staff. Some would wear the office wallpaper if they thought it would add to their air of discretion. Others, like the security staff, blended in effortlessly as their role demanded. Amanda was one of those supremely confident women who occupied her physical space in a room in a manner that attracted rather than deflected attention. With her long auburn tresses and sharply carved features, she reminded David of the figurehead on a ship's prow, cutting her way through the corridors of Globe Oil's British headquarters as people flowed about her to right and left, unconsciously making way. David gave a small smile, pleased with his analogy. Out of the corner of his eye, he saw the time displayed on the corner of his computer screen. 8 p.m. Amanda was smiling back at him so he held the expression, adding a friendly nod that he hoped would convey suitable appreciation for her professionalism. Like all the other beautiful, intelligent women who crossed his path, she left him cold.

'Let's leave it there,' he said, pleasantly. 'I don't think there's anything else that can't wait until Monday, Amanda.'

'Right, sir. Thank you.' David slid a bundle of documents into his desk drawer and stood, his mind already on the draft of an after-dinner speech he'd be revising later that evening. The half-tilted blinds on the office window let the evening sun slant through in ribbons, illuminating tiny dust particles dancing in the air. When their daughter was young, Carlotta used to tell her it was angel dust. He could certainly use a bit of that, he thought, lifting his hand into the light, fingers splayed to maximize the possibility of making contact. It didn't work. Carlotta would have laughed at him. *Il sognatore*, she'd have teased. Dreamer. David's hand fell to his side. Dreams were hard to hold onto, especially once you had them in the palm of your hand. It was then, when you felt safe, that they were most at risk of slipping away, like angel dust.

'What about dinner?' he mumbled, doing a quick mental scan of his refrigerator. There was a ready meal in his freezer box, glammed up with fancy packaging and a posh product description but in the final analysis, still a ready meal. He was fairly certain there was a bag of salad cowering on one of the back shelves as well. Yes, that would do.

'I'd be delighted.'

'I'm sorry?' Turning, David found Amanda Webster still in the room, waiting to be officially dismissed. There was a look of utter triumph on her face.

'I'd be delighted.' She smoothed an imagined crease from her blue pencil skirt and blushed prettily. 'Sir,' she added, remembering his position. 'I never imagined for a second that you'd ask, but I . . . well, I hoped you might, one day.'

'I . . . er . . . that's very flattering. Really?' In his mind's eye, David saw himself as a damaged fighter jet, plummeting earthwards and picking up speed.

'Of course, who wouldn't?' Amanda picked up her over-sized leather handbag and looped the strap over her shoulder.

'Well, I wouldn't presume . . .' *Abort, abort!* Was it possible to save himself?

'Although most men ask me out sooner or later,' she cut across him, her tone not boastful but matter-of-fact, 'so I suppose I shouldn't feel all that surprised.'

David looked around wildly. The advantage of fighter jets over corporate offices was, he decided, the eject button facility. This was excruciating. He took a deep breath.

'Look, Amanda, Ms Webster. I'm terribly sorry but you seem to have –' At that moment the phone rang. David flung himself towards it and snatched up the receiver. 'Hello? Yes, speaking.' He listened intently for a few seconds, then said, 'We can certainly discuss that. No, I have time, but would you excuse me for a moment?' Laying the phone gently on the desk, he offered Amanda his most apologetic smile. She was loitering by the door, one hand resting jauntily on her hip. 'I'm sorry, this conversation needs to be private. I don't want to hold you up.'

'Oh, you're not. Shall I wait in my office?'

'I'll be some time. It's the prime minister, um, er, sustainable energy crisis.'

Her smile faltered a little. 'I don't mind waiting.'

'Please, I insist.'

Amanda flushed, finally recognizing the snub. She turned on her heel and tugged the door open. 'Enjoy your weekend,' she said, caustically. 'Sir.' David winced as the door slammed behind her, causing a rather expensive painting to judder on the wall. He raised his eyes heavenwards, imagining the story passing from office to office in an increasingly mangled, whispered form, until it ended up that he had hit on Amanda and she had spurned his advances. With a heavy sigh, David retrieved the phone.

'Rich? Sorry about that.'

'Beating them off with a stick, are you?'

'Just an unfortunate misunderstanding.'

'Certainly sounded that way,' Rich agreed. 'I take it she's gone?'

'Possibly permanently.' David heard the sound of muted chatter in the background. 'Where are you?'

'In the pub. Beth's got a meeting. Why the prime minister, by the way?'

'First thing that came to mind,' replied David, flopping into his chair and rubbing his eyes. 'It was either that or leap into the cupboard and say I was popping through to Narnia.' He grinned at the shout of laughter that came through the receiver. 'It's great to hear your voice, mate. We only ever seem to catch up over the board table these days. How's married life?'

'Top-notch. That's why I'm ringing. Any chance of getting together so you can finally meet her?'

Chapter Four

Beth was up to her elbows in dishwater when there was a tap at the kitchen window around 11:30. Her enormous yawn became a squawk of fright as her husband's face appeared on the other side of the glass. 'Rich! You scared me.' He mouthed something she couldn't make out. 'What?' He repeated the message. 'What are you . . . oh, right.' She wiped her hands on her jeans and stuck her head out of the back door. 'All clear,' she announced. 'Janet has left the building.' Rich emerged from behind the rose bush and scuttled for safety. 'Some tough guy you are,' said Beth wryly, lifting her face for his kiss.

'Wait a second.' He dodged past her and did a quick check of the lounge and stairs. 'OK. Building is secure.'

'What, you think I'd hide her in there for a joke?'

'Yes,' he said, frankly. 'And don't say you haven't considered it.'

'OK,' she grinned, wickedly. 'I won't.'

'I knew it.' He swooped without warning and grabbed her in a rib-cracking hug.

'Stop!' she shrieked, flailing her arms and legs. 'I can't breathe.'

'Say you're sorry.'

'But I didn't do it!'

'Fair point,' he admitted, letting her slide down in his arms far enough to kiss her.

'Ugh, you taste all beery.'

'Tough. I love you.' Rich kissed her again before letting her squirm free. 'How did it go? They liked your idea?'

'Great, thanks. I think they might run with it. Janet's really not that bad, you know.'

'You're not the one she hits on,' he retorted, flicking the kettle on and choosing a pair of mugs from the draining board. 'Is there any flapjack left?' he asked hopefully.

'There was, but . . .'

'But?' he prompted.

'Janet's little dog got into the kitchen and ate it.'

'That woman is the bane of my life.'

'I thought that was me?'

He laughed. 'No rule saying I can't have two.' He slam-dunked the tea bags into the mugs and stretched wearily. 'Go on up, love, I'll bring these. You look tired.'

'Mm.' Beth started inching towards the lounge door, her body carefully angled away from him.

'What are you doing?'

'Mmph?'

'You look like you're creeping up on someone.' Her shoulders started to shake, but she kept her face turned away. In a flash, he realized. Creeping *away*, not creeping up.

'Be-eth . . .'

She spun round, cheeks bulging with the flapjack she'd crammed in. Tears of silent laughter were spilling down her face.

'Was that the last piece?' he demanded. She nodded. 'Right.' He put the milk carton down with a thump. 'Now you're in for it.' Beth bolted for the stairs and he charged after her, yelling, 'No mercy!' The mugs of tea stood forgotten on the worktop, steaming gently and wondering who had switched their sensible adult drinkers for howling teenagers.

Fifty miles away, another mug sat waiting in a different kitchen, a primed cafetiere by its side. The mug was so big that it was more of a bowl, the kind the French used for hot chocolate. An old-fashioned whistle kettle squatted on a gas hob, preparing to scream as the water boiled. A broad work surface ran around the room's perimeter, spanning three of the rectangular room's four walls. The flow was interrupted on one wall by an American-style refrigerator and a cavernous Belfast sink that could bath two children, and again by a large double oven on the wall opposite. Shelves and utensil racks mirrored the work surface above and below, and an enormous stainless steel table covered most of the central floor space, hiding much of the red-tiled floor. Cerys would have preferred a wooden table, but steel was easier to clean and gave the required nod to health and safety. The fourth wall bore simple adornments – a brick kiln in pride of place at the head of the room and a plain whitewashed wooden door in the corner, connecting the kitchen to the patisserie-cum-bakery that Cerys had proudly christened 'Rise', ignoring all objections to the pun.

The door flew open and Cerys entered at a run as the kettle began to whistle, a broom clutched in one hand and a dustpan in the other. She propped them against the table, snatched the kettle from its perch and filled the cafetiere to the brim. When she went to fetch a jug of cream from the fridge, her hand hovered briefly over a second cup before falling away. There was no point. Martin might be back in fifteen minutes or not for another hour, depending on traffic and how well his last sales meeting had gone. He drove faster when he was in a bad mood. In that respect, the fact that he was late was probably a good sign. Cerys delved into the striped pocket of her apron and pulled out her mobile. No message yet. She dragged a high stool out from beneath the table and hiked herself onto it with a sigh. The blue paint on the spindle-style legs was badly chipped in a number of places, but she didn't think it worth repainting. She had bought a set of four from a flea market years ago, and this was the last survivor. Besides, nobody ever saw it except Cerys and her two staff, Rico and Emma. Like her, they were only interested in the baking.

Cerys took a swig of coffee, holding the liquid in her mouth for a few seconds until the strong flavour had saturated her tongue. She took a deep breath, held it and then exhaled, allowing herself to relax. The shop was all closed up and cleaned, 4-year-old Phoebe was sound asleep in the spacious flat above the bakery and might even sleep through the night – Cerys's hand brushed against the seat of the wooden stool for luck – and since Martin wasn't home yet, she had a rare pocket of time to call her own. Time spent asleep didn't count since she wasn't awake to enjoy it, and she got precious little of it in any case. Cerys had another drink of coffee, cupping the mug greedily in both hands. After a busy day, silence truly did have a golden quality. Even as the thought crossed her mind, the phone rang. Cerys groaned and reluctantly pressed the answer button.

'Hello?'

'Not in bed yet, darling?'

'No, Mum. Just finished clearing up.'

'At half past eleven? You need more staff.' Her mother sounded full of energy, more like 30 than 78. The relentless upbeat manner that had been the hallmark of Cerys's and Beth's childhood was as wearing as ever.

'I can't afford it, Mum.' Cerys pushed a hand through the dark mop of hair that sprang in thick, unruly curls about her head, semi-tamed into a rough bob. 'Anyway,' she yawned, 'I enjoy tidying up. It's a nice full stop to the day.'

'Four years and you can't afford more staff. I suppose it's the recession. How's Phoebe?' As usual, the subject changes were deft and disconnected.

'Asleep,' Cerys said, her brain scrambling to keep up.

'I must pop down and see you soon.'

'Lovely. Drop in anytime, Mum. I'm always here.'

'Well, naturally. Where else would you be, darling? Right, speak soon.' The conversation closed as abruptly as it had begun.

'Mum? Hang on!'

'Yes?'

'Don't call Beth tonight, will you? She's had that meeting, so she'll be dead tired.' And Rich is at home so don't interrupt their time, she pleaded silently.

'I might be old, darling, but I'm not senile. Don't teach your mother to suck eggs. Goodnight!'

The phone went dead. Cerys held it away from her and stared at it, as though the handset were somehow responsible for the staccato, disjointed conversation. 'Right. Bye then, Mum,' she sighed, making a mental note to speak to Beth. Mum clearly needed another hobby, preferably one that would tire her out so she would stop hounding her children at midnight. Cerys raised her face to the ceiling as a muffled thump came from upstairs, followed by a piercing cry. 'Damn,' she swore quietly. She drained her mug of coffee, slid off the stool and made for the stairs.

Back in the cottage, Rich sat up in bed with a start. 'I completely forgot the tea,' he said, mournfully. 'Do you want a fresh one?'

'Ooh, yes please.' Beth hid her face in the pillow to smother her giggles as he left the room, muttering, 'Waste of a good brew, that was.' Her husband kept himself in remarkably good shape physically, but inside him there was an old man clamouring to get out.

'And some cheese?' she called after him. 'Midnight feast!' His snort of disgust carried back up the stairs. Rich ate biscuits in bed. Beth ate cheese, no biscuits. She rolled onto her back and grinned up at the ceiling, where dark beams criss-crossed the room like railway sleepers. Things were wonderful when Rich was at home. It was like being encased in a warm bubble where nothing could touch her. Then there'd be a phone call and the bubble would burst abruptly, the inrush of cold air carrying Rich away on another infernal business trip, leaving her alone and shivering. Sometimes it was only a week but more often a month, six weeks. He was so diligent, never leaving until he was sure the job was done properly. That was why they sent him. It was also why Beth had insisted they live in her place instead of Rich's stupidly large house in Thames Ditton. There, she had wandered from room to empty room in his absence, each one spotlessly clean, untouched and lonelier than the last. And cold, always cold. Sometimes she'd messed them all up, throwing cushions off the sofas and scattering ornaments across the carpets and coffee tables, just to create signs of life. The cleaner would eye her sideways on the occasions when they'd bumped into each other on the doorstep, clearly wondering what kind of wild parties Mrs Hampton indulged in while the master was away. Here in the cottage she was cosy, the bare walls cushioned with old black and white photos and modern prints in wacky frames, odds and ends crammed into every inch of space and the little log-burning stove wrapping everything in comforting heat.

Ever easygoing, Rich had sold up without a murmur, crammed what he could into the cottage and put the rest into storage. 'I just want to be where you are,' he'd said with a shrug when she'd tearfully thanked him for the sacrifice. Beth thought he secretly preferred the village of Little Bookham to Thames Ditton. Here, they were still more or less in the commuter belt for London, but without the essential veneer of keeping up with the neighbours that seemed to coat even the pavements of Thames Ditton. The people were pleasant enough, but Beth had felt judged in a thousand subtle ways, simply for wanting to be herself. No one had condemned her in any obvious manner; it was more like being surrounded by a constant cloud of polite but ever-present confusion. People just didn't 'get' her. Rich hadn't understood that part, but of course, he wouldn't. His face already fitted. Beth heard his footsteps on the stairs and pushed herself up in bed, discarding the negative thought spiral. No point dwelling on the lonely times. He was here now, and that was what mattered.

'Here you go,' Rich said, edging the door open with his foot, and slipping in with a tea tray. He balanced it on the bedside table and hopped back into bed. Beth reached over him, and grabbed the plate of mixed cheese.

'Yum.'

'Savage,' he accused her, dunking a pair of biscuits into his drink.

'What?' she protested. 'Nobody really *likes* cheese biscuits, you know. It's just for the look of it. People only want the cheese.' She didn't really believe this, but ditching the biscuits meant less crumbs and gave her the moral high ground when they had to get up and do a sheet-sweep at 3 a.m.

'I like them,' Rich objected.

'Yes, and you'd dunk them in your tea at work, given half a chance.' Beth laughed. 'I can't see that going down too well at one of your stuffed-shirt business dinners, can you?'

'No,' he agreed, fingers closing absentmindedly over his next two biscuits as he swallowed the first batch. 'But it would almost be worth it to see their faces.' His face lit up and he turned towards her, almost upsetting the tea tray. Beth lunged for the teapot just in time, one hand curving protectively around her precious cheese.

'Watch it.'

'Sorry.' He repositioned the tray on his knees. 'Crisis over,' he grinned. 'I was going to say, I managed to get David on the phone tonight.'

'Really?' Beth's heart sank. 'Another business trip?'

'No,' he smiled, smoothing the worry from her face with a gentle hand. 'For a chat.'

'A chat? David?'

'We do catch up occasionally, love.'

'Yes, but we've been married almost a year now and I still haven't met the guy.' And he's supposed to be one of your best friends, she added silently. 'I know he works, like, twenty-two hours a day,' she finished lamely, not wanting to sound churlish.

'He wasn't always like that,' said Rich, holding her gaze in a way that told her he knew what she was thinking.

'I know,' she mumbled, suddenly awash with shame at her meanness. 'Carlotta.' David's wife sounded like some kind of all-singing, all-dancing superwoman who was not only stunningly gorgeous, but also remembered the birthdays of everyone she'd ever met and always had dinner ready on time. When Rich spoke of her, there was a tinge of reverence to his voice. Beth didn't like that either, and felt mean all over again. In an effort to redress the balance she said, 'We'd have met at his daughter's wedding if I hadn't been working, so I'm just as bad.' Rich was watching her steadily, familiar with these bouts of internal wrestling.

'All I was going to say,' he said, shuffling across the mattress and depositing the tea tray on the carpet, 'was that we managed to find a couple of potential dates for dinner.'

'A business dinner?' she said, suspiciously. Above all other things, she loathed corporate dinners where she was obliged to make polite conversation with various fat cats and their emaciated, preening wives.

'No,' he replied, lying down with a sigh and pulling her along with him. 'Nothing fancy, maybe a sushi bar after work.'

'Just the three of us? No Stepford Wives?'

'Promise. Check your work diary in the morning.' He glanced at the LED display on the clock radio and groaned. 'It's half past one. Time for sleep.' Beth freed one arm to flick the light off and settled down, Rich's long limbs tucked round her like a human blanket. Then her phone rang, shattering the silence with all the subtlety of a brick through a window. Rich jumped violently, his body virtually clearing the mattress.

'What the – !'

'Sorry, sorry.' Beth fumbled for the phone beneath her pillow. 'Hello? Mum?'

'Are you in bed?'

'Um, yes.'

'Oh, sorry, darling. Must have lost track of time.' Beth scrunched her eyes shut as her mother's voice boomed through the handset. Rich rolled over and stuck his head under the pillow. 'I just wanted to know how your meeting went.'

'It was good, really exciting. We, um, got a lot done.' Beth stifled a yawn. 'Mum, can I call you tomorrow? I'll tell you all about it then. Rich has an early start.'

'Of course, darling.' Her mother's voice was so bright and breezy it could have been the middle of the day. She never needed much sleep. 'Night-night, then.'

'Oh, Mum? Mum?' Beth said hurriedly, panicking as a thought struck her.

'Still here.'

'Don't call Cerys just now, will you? Only, she'll be up in a couple of hours and . . .'

A sigh gusted down the phone. 'Credit me with *some* sense, Elizabeth. Good night.'

'Night, Mum.' She dropped the phone onto the floor and buried her head in the duvet. 'Don't say it.'

'I didn't,' came the muffled reply.

'I heard you thinking it.'

'Are we going to get *any* sleep tonight?'

Slumped against the side of Phoebe's bed, Cerys was wondering the same thing.

'Mummy?'

'Still here, poppet.'

'Can you sing it for me again?'

'Not again, Phoebe. Mummy's really tired.'

'But the bad dream's still in my head. Sing it out for me, Mummy?'

Cerys reached out to stroke her daughter's soft curls. 'Last time, then,' she said, digging deep for the last scraps of energy and patience. The usual reserves were long gone. Leaning her head against the edge of the mattress, she murmured the old lullaby from her childhood, stumbling over the words in her exhaustion. Phoebe's bad dreams were becoming a regular fixture lately. Shadows on the wall, the creak of a floorboard, the wind in the trees – any of these were enough to set off a chain of thoughts that left her trembling beneath the covers. When she finally nodded off, the fear seemed to poison her sleep. Phoebe's subconscious was nothing if not thorough; so far they'd had monster under the bed, in the cupboard, at the window, nasty trees, and snakes. The current fear was of being stolen away. Cerys suspected Phoebe had caught a snippet of a child abduction story on the radio, but she couldn't be sure. Phoebe refused to discuss her bad dreams in the daytime and there was little point in trying to cross-examine a sweat-drenched, sobbing 4-year-old in the middle of the night. 'She'll grow out of it,' Martin had said, brushing the subject off when Cerys raised it. 'All children go through it.'

'I didn't,' Cerys objected.

'I thought you had a recurring nightmare about burning your grandma's cakes, and not being able to get the oven door open to save them?'

'That was just a dream. They were Victoria sponges, not killer cakes. I never had nightmares.'

'Then you're the exception that proves the rule,' he'd replied, firmly. Case closed.

All very well for him, Cerys thought now, her knees clicking painfully as she eased herself off the floor, trying not to lean on the mattress. Martin slept like the dead and rarely heard Phoebe's cries. Cerys was the one who had to deal with the fallout. She backed slowly out of the room, still singing softly, and pulled the door to. It was dark on the landing, but she could just make out the time on her wristwatch. Quarter to two. She'd have to be up at 5:30 to bake the bread for her morning customers. Cerys heard the front door close downstairs and knew Martin was home, but she couldn't summon the strength to trot down and greet him as she usually did when his clattering arrival woke her up. Then she realized she hadn't texted Beth to see how her meeting had gone. 'Bad wife, daughter *and* sister,' she yawned. 'A bumper night.' Sometimes she just couldn't cover all the bases, no matter how hard she tried. With a sigh of pure exhaustion, Cerys tottered into her bedroom and fell into bed. It could wait until the morning. They could all wait until morning.

Chapter Five

Beth was playing the Train Game. As teenagers, she and Cerys took the train to school every day, leaving their little village for the comparatively bright lights of the nearest town and the dubious pleasures of its local comprehensive. Their parents could have afforded any of the public schools for their girls, but that would have offended their 'right-on' political views. 'If the state system is good enough for Paul McCartney's children, it's good enough for you,' their father stated flatly in response to their pleas, well aware of his daughters' true motivations. Neither Cerys nor Beth cared about the standard of their education; Beth liked the summer straw boaters and dramatic winter capes of the uniforms at their nearest public school, while Cerys harboured an early fixation with rugby players, and wanted to play lacrosse.

When they grew tired of reading their books or dissecting the latest playground gossip on their daily journey, they would each pick a fellow passenger at random and invent a life story for them, tearing a page from the back of an exercise book and scribbling furiously. Name, age, job and destination came first, followed by family background, friends, relatives and anything else that came to mind. The rule was one page only. Then they would swap notes and sit sniggering at the wild stories they'd invented. Beth still played the Train Game occasionally while en route to London for

work, though only in her head. It was less fun without
Cerys, but sufficiently amusing to pass the time.

Today she had a meeting about a prospective photo shoot
for an up and coming clothes range, followed by a quick ren-
dezvous with Cerys for lunch. The Train Game victim was
an elderly lady sitting diagonally across the aisle from Beth.
Engrossed in a novel, she was unaware of Beth's scrutiny.
Beth estimated that she was in her eighties, and beautiful, or
had certainly been so in her youth. Her trained photographer's eye traced the bone structure of the lady's face. Beneath
the crumpled, tissue-paper skin of her face were elegantly
high cheekbones, a high, proud forehead and a strong jaw.
Beth fancied there was a touch of melancholy about the
woman and craned her neck a little to get a look at the
hands. No wedding ring. A jilted bride, perhaps? Or – far
better – a fiancé killed in action during the Second World
War. Yes. Beth gave a satisfied nod. Cerys would approve of
the drama of it. Narrowing her eyes, she studied the woman
even more closely, noting the neat, precise movements as she
turned the pages of her book, or lifted her insulated thermos
mug to her lips. Now and again she raised her head to look
around the carriage with eyes that were still bright and alert.

Beth stifled a gasp of delight as the woman lifted her book
slightly, revealing the cover. Voltaire. *Yes.* It all fitted. She had
been a spy, trained by the SAS and parachuted into France to
work alongside the Resistance, where her French lover had
been tragically killed, ooh, a couple of days before the war
ended? And on a mission that he was not intended to take
part in. The woman had returned to England heartbroken
and, despite many suitors over the years, had remained a

spinster. No man had ever quite measured up to . . . Beth paused, searching for the right name . . . Claude? Michel? No, too common. Something more special. *Sebastian*. And the lady's name was Vivian, which would have sounded well in French, *Vivienne*. Beth was thoroughly enjoying herself now, her own book lying forgotten on her lap.

'Excuse me.' The man in the window seat next to her began to get up, gathering his coat and briefcase.

'Of course.' Beth squeezed into the aisle to let the man out as the train slowed with a screech of brakes. She moved over into the vacant window seat and settled down, preparing for the next instalment of Vivian's tragedy-scarred life. The train set off again with a lurch and Beth closed her eyes for a moment, trying to conjure an image of 'the final good-bye' in her mind.

'Is this seat taken?' Beth ignored the voice, determined to hold her focus. 'Excuse me, is this seat taken?'

Reluctantly, Beth opened her eyes. 'No, it's free,' she said to the newcomer hovering in the aisle. Immediately she closed her eyes again, dismissing the passenger's existence, though the man's elbow bumped her arm several times as he shuffled about beside her, trying to get comfortable. Beth retracted her arm but the man's arm followed. She shifted irritably but the arm remained where it was. Clearly he was one of those travellers who expanded to fit the available space, rather than maintaining the maximum possible personal distance from others on public transport. Worse still, when Beth opened her eyes she found that the man had plonked a laptop onto the little pull-down table set into the seat in front, and was completely blocking her view of

Vivian. Beth tutted, more audibly than she intended. Instantly, the man's head swung round.

'I'm sorry, am I in your way at all?' he asked, politely.

'No,' Beth muttered, ungraciously. 'Carry on.' She folded her arms and stared out of the window, thoroughly disgruntled. After a few seconds, she became aware that the stranger was still looking at her. 'Can I help you?' she asked, turning a cold stare on him.

'No, er . . . no. Forgive me.' The man looked embarrassed and began fiddling with his laptop.

As soon as Beth turned away, his eyes were drawn back to her. He couldn't help it. David swallowed hard. She was so beautiful.

At that moment, a people carrier was crawling along the M25 in the direction of Heathrow. The back of the car was taken up with luggage, and three bulky, padded child seats were squeezed into the middle section with barely a finger width between them, much like the traffic outside. Nathan peered into the distance and shook his head. 'Bumper to bumper from here to the horizon,' he said, glumly. 'You shouldn't have come, love.'

'Nonsense,' said Jenny, briskly. 'We want to see you safely off.' Especially since there'll be precious little safety where you're headed, she thought, quashing her rising anxiety for what felt like the hundredth time since breakfast. Every moment with Nathan was precious.

'We'll be stuck here for hours.'

'We left in good time,' Jenny replied, evenly. 'You'll make the flight.' Nathan reached over to take her hand.

'I'm not worried about that,' he said quietly, obviously aware that Abigail's ears would be revolving like twin satellite dishes from her seat in the back. 'I don't want to swan off at the airport and leave you with a long journey back and three cranky you-know-whos to deal with. I'll feel terribly guilty.'

'Don't be silly.' Jenny bit back her initial response, which was to say that she mostly dealt with the children on her own every day, cranky or not. A job was a job, and Nathan couldn't pick and choose his working hours, or the places he was sent. There were no strings he could pull. David could, though. Jenny recalled the moment her hand had hovered over the telephone after she'd heard the news, poised to ring David and beg him to send someone else to Kazakhstan to oversee the state of the company's interests in the development of a new gas field called Karachaganak. Even the name sounded violent. She must have stood there for at least quarter of an hour before she could force her hand away from the receiver. There was no point asking. David was too scrupulously fair to even consider favouring a friend, and Nathan would never forgive her for making such a request. There was nothing to be done but grin and bear it. And pray. She smiled at her husband, trying to erase all trace of her thoughts from her eyes. 'You're hardly swanning off, Nathan,' she pointed out. 'It's not a holiday. You'd get more rest at home.'

Nathan squeezed her hand. She knew he was grateful for the generosity of her white lie. 'What did I ever do to deserve such an amazing wife?'

'I don't know,' she replied. 'But it must have been really good.' Nathan leaned over to kiss her, but leapt back like a guilty teenager as the car behind them honked its horn. 'For crying out loud!' he tutted, shifting the car into first gear and crawling forward as the traffic ahead began to move. 'Is it really worth getting hot under the collar for the sake of two metres?'

'Don't get worked up,' Jenny warned. 'Or you'll fall into the same trap as him.'

'OK, OK.' Nathan swore under his breath – but not quietly enough.

'What did Daddy say?' Abigail piped up.

'You don't need to know,' Jenny said swiftly, shaking her head as Nathan mouthed an apology.

'But I want to know.'

'Well, you can't, darling. Not yet.'

'When can I know?'

'When you're older.'

'How old?'

'Thirty-six,' Nathan put in unwisely.

'But that's aaaages!' Abigail howled. Jenny bit her tongue and looked out of the window, determined not to point out that meltdown could have been avoided. Abigail's cries woke Rory, who immediately added his voice to hers.

'There yet, Mummy?' asked Michael. 'There yet?'

'No, sweetheart,' she said through gritted teeth. 'But you're being very good.'

'Sorry, Jen.' Nathan rammed a CD into the machine and hit the play button. 'The wheels on the bus' belted out of the speakers and reverberated round the packed car. Jenny closed her eyes wearily.

'Forget it. They'll sleep on the way home.'

On the train to London, the woman sitting next to David was also wearing an expression of profound weariness. Or maybe she was irritated at having to share the space with him. His briefcase was wedged between his feet, causing his knees to splay out, and his laptop seemed to be taking up more space than it usually did. David scowled at the compact screen, trying to prevent himself from stealing occasional glances at the woman by immersing himself in quarterly growth figures. Trying – and failing repeatedly. She was breathtaking, from the clear complexion and natural glow of her skin, to the waterfall of blonde hair tumbling past her face. She was staring out of the window with a fixed expression, one hand tugging at the tips of her hair. On her finger a diamond engagement ring sparkled beside the quiet elegance of a wedding band, the message plain for all to see: 'I'm taken.' Still David stared, embarrassed but unable to stop himself. He told himself that it was just curiosity, detached appreciation of such rare, natural beauty. Feverishly, his brain catalogued her every feature even as he struggled to ignore her presence. Her colouring was pale, her eyes light blue, the skin on her hands almost translucent. The fingers twisting the ends of her hair were long and slender, tapering to short, square-cut nails. Encased in plain stonewashed denim, her legs were long, the tips of red leather ballet pumps peeping out beneath the hem of her jeans. She would be tall – six foot, maybe more. A blue tear-shaped pendant was visible at the open neck of her red and white polka-dot cotton blouse, a kind of semi-precious stone he didn't recognize. Above it David detected the woman's pulse beating her life's rhythm in the delicate hollow of her throat. He swallowed and tore his gaze away from her as she shifted in her seat, cursing himself for such stupid behaviour. There were beautiful women all around him, working in the office, at parties, meetings, strangers on the street. None of them moved him, and he had begun to think that no one ever could, after Carlotta. What quality did this woman have that they didn't? She was just a woman in jeans and a short-sleeved shirt, the little capped sleeves emphasising the toned muscles of her upper arms. As far as he could tell, she wore no make-up, no nail polish, her hair was loose and unstyled. She wasn't even particularly young. Thirties? He guessed, flushing as she suddenly turned towards him as though reading his thoughts.

'Excuse me,' she said.

His throat was dry. 'Yes?'

'I need to get out, please.'

'Oh, right.' He scrambled to his feet, clutching the laptop to his chest. 'This is your stop. Sorry.'

She stared at him for a moment with an expression that hinted at pity. 'It's everybody's stop. Waterloo.' She gestured out of the window at the approaching station as the carriage juddered and all around them people began to stand and gather their belongings. 'End of the line.'

'So it is,' David said, forcing a smile onto his burning face. 'Too caught up in work.' He tapped the laptop, staggering slightly as a man with a large rucksack jostled him in the aisle. 'Please.' He moved back and the woman sidestepped past him, turning to pull a large, black canvas bag from the luggage rack. David felt a jolt go through him as her arm brushed against his. She half-turned and he held his breath, wondering if she had felt the connection as he did.

'Thanks.' Heaving the bag onto her shoulder, she left the train without a backwards glance. David's heart sank into his shoes. He shuffled back into the empty seat space as other passengers hurried to leave the train, his knees bent at an awkward angle against the edge of the chair. He stuffed his laptop into its case and retrieved his briefcase from under the seat. First-class had much to recommend it in terms of comfort and space. But it didn't have her.

David raised his head and looked out of the carriage window, hoping for a last glimpse. She was on the platform, embracing a petite girl with a mop of dark curls that made her head look twice its actual size. The woman gestured back at the train and turned her head towards him. For a brief second, their eyes met and there it was again, that inexplicable feeling of connection. Then David was ducking out of sight, his embarrassment now complete. When he left the train, the crowd had swallowed the beautiful stranger and he was alone. *Who was she?* 'She was married, you fool,' he sighed. Not that it mattered whether she was or she wasn't. She was just a woman on a train, who he'd never see again. David caught sight of the station clock and pulled out his mobile. He wanted to catch Nathan before his flight left, wish him good luck.

'Who was that man?' Cerys asked as the sisters stood side by side on the Tube platform, a rush of warm, stale air lifting her curls as a full train flashed past. 'The one watching you from the window.'

Beth shrugged dismissively, though her heart was jumping like a frightened animal. 'No idea. He was next to me on the train. Weird guy. He kept staring at me.'

'Why?'

'Dunno. I was playing the Train Game until he got in the way.' A half-remembered image flashed into her mind, but was gone before she could capture it. 'I think I've seen him before somewhere, actually.' She frowned. 'A photo, or . . . an article, maybe.' Did she know him? There'd been something in the way he'd looked at her . . . had it been recognition, or the hope of knowing her better? She shivered, turning her attention back to her sister.

'That'll be it,' said Cerys cheerfully. 'He was probably an old colleague not wanting to bother you but hoping you'd recognize him and say hello.'

'Oh, I hope not.' Beth felt an odd disappointment at the thought that Cerys might be right.

'Bet he thinks you're unbelievably rude.'

'Thanks, Cerys.' Beth made a show of checking her watch. 'Maybe I don't have time for that coffee after all. Do your own market research on your business rivals.' There were plans to extend Rise and incorporate a café, but Cerys was still in two minds about it. Cerys grinned and linked her arm through Beth's. 'OK, I'll be nice,' she promised. 'No need to take a huff.'

'I wasn't.'

'Uh-huh.' Cerys looked down at her feet in an unsuccessful attempt to hide her smirk.

'Cerys!'

'What? Chill out. Maybe he didn't know you. He probably fancied you.'

Beth stepped back as the next train clattered through the tunnel. 'Shut up and get on, would you?'

'There's no need to be embarrassed. You're still pretty hot for an old bird.'

'Move it before I push you onto the track.'

'Some people are so touchy!' They squeezed into the carriage, the sound of their easy bickering cut off by the closing doors.

Chapter Six

It was a hot day, even for August. Hot outdoors and sweltering inside. Cerys dabbed at her forehead with a baby wipe, binned it and automatically reached for the pump and spray sanitizing hand gel. She had once tried to estimate how many times a day she used it in the shop, and decided it was around a hundred. No wonder her hands looked like her mother's, she thought, eyeing the sore, dry patches on her knuckles. She leaned on the counter, her arms like a protective shield over the clear glass top. The cabinet beneath housed a family of cakes and speciality breads that were drawing more customers than ever. Better yet, the regulars weren't being put off by the tourists, something Cerys feared every summer.

Cerys was proud of Rise. Something told her it was going to be a bumper season. She looked longingly at the apple, blackcurrant and clotted cream cupcakes nestled happily between a row of strawberry tarts and miniature chocolate chip brioches. Only 1 o'clock and there were hardly any left. It was tempting to put one behind the counter for her afternoon snack but after a brief struggle, she chose a cherry and walnut scone. They were cheaper to make and less attractive than the cupcakes. 'Window-dressing is vital,' she reminded herself, her mouth still watering at the thought of the tangy blackcurrant on her tongue. She gazed out of the window, watching the children roaming the pebbly beach in packs, wearing their sunhats askew on their heads and their sunblock cream in warpainted stripes on their faces. The parents appeared to fall into two categories – bikini-clad mothers, glazed with bronzing oil and topped with large floppy sunhats, and tired mums in shorts and T-shirts, loaded up with buckets, spades and bottled water, and peppered with heat rash or sunburn. Both categories had striped deckchairs, but that seemed to be the only common ground between them.

Cerys winced at the thought of the trains travelling back to the city at the end of the day. Overcrowding would be putting it mildly. Brighton was a classic destination for London day trippers. They arrived in a rush with the midmorning sun, swept over the beach and the marina and ebbed away at dusk, like a human tidal wave. Only in the summer was the beach engulfed, but there was a steady stream of visitors to Brighton throughout the year. It had an easygoing vibe that was all its own, and Cerys loved it.

The kitchen door opened and Rico stuck his head through. He had been working for Cerys for two years now, supplementing his student loan with regular shifts. Cerys had taught him an awful lot in that time and he, in return, brought in a great deal of trade from the university by word of mouth. 'OK in here?'

'Yes, you're fine, Rico,' Cerys replied, indicating the empty shop with a lazy wave. 'You guys finish your lunch. I'll call if there's a rush.'

'OK, great.' He gave the thumbs-up to Emma through the open door, and disappeared into the kitchen. Cerys's first-ever member of staff, Emma, worked full-time in the shop and had quickly become a right-hand woman. If business stayed strong, Cerys hoped to sponsor her to attend catering college part-time. She had a light, natural touch, and was improving all the time. Cerys strolled over to the window and returned to people-watching. If only they would stay still for a while she could play the Train Game, she thought idly, wondering if it could be adapted to a shifting crowd.

The bell on the door jamb pinged, announcing customers. Cerys looked up in surprise as a woman elbowed her way into the shop with a double buggy, a small girl trailing mutinously behind on foot. Breakfast, mid-morning and mid-afternoon were their busy times of day. Lunch was their fallow time. The woman had a friendly, capable manner, but she looked tired – long-term tired. Her shoulders slumped as if beneath layers of fatigue, worn like heavy winter clothes.

'Hi there,' Cerys said, straightening her polka-dot apron and moving back to the counter. 'What can I get you?'

The woman smiled. 'So much to choose from,' she commented, eyeing the wide range of cakes in the cooler cabinet. 'Perhaps a cupcake for the children and . . .' She hesitated, her brow wrinkling over the decision. '. . . I think I'd quite like a scone.' She looked suddenly anxious. 'Is that terribly boring of me?'

'Not at all,' Cerys lied, picking up the long-handled silver serving tongs. The little girl had her face pressed up to the cabinet, making sticky imprints on the glass. Cerys slid the cakes into a paper bag with a practised hand, and passed them over the counter. The woman dipped into her purse. 'How much does that come to?'

'It'll be £4.25, please.'

The woman scrabbled about for a few seconds before handing over the exact change. Cerys smiled and nodded her thanks. When she turned back from the till the woman was still standing there, clutching the bag. There was an awkward silence, then she said, 'I'm not sure I've come to the right place.'

'Oh?'

'You are Cerys, aren't you? I'm Jenny. Jenny Creston.'

'Er . . .' Cerys's face remained politely blank. Jenny Creston. Wait, there was something . . . the machinery of her brain gave several internal clunks as the information thudded into place. She clapped a hand to her head. 'Oh, I'm so sorry,' she gasped. 'You're Rich Hampton's friend, aren't you? Beth did ring me and I clean forgot. It's the early mornings, they're such a killer . . .' she stopped with an effort, realizing she'd gone into babble mode. Beth had told her Jenny and her family were coming down to Brighton, and had asked if they could meet up with Cerys and Phoebe for an hour, since Jenny's daughter was the same age. Jenny laughed.

'Tell me about it,' she said, visibly relaxing. 'We have a lot of those in our house.'

'I bet.' Cerys gestured at the bag of cakes. 'Listen, you should have introduced yourself sooner. Let me give you a refund for those.'

'Certainly not.' Jenny whipped out the scone and quickly bit into it. 'I've heard about this place,' she mumbled, 'and you should raise your prices. This is heavenly.'

'Well, thanks,' Cerys said, pleased by the compliment. 'But the next ones are on the house.'

'No arguments there,' Jenny said through her second mouthful. They shared a smile, each experiencing the silent recognition that sometimes passes between strangers: *Yes, we're going to be friends.* Jenny looked questioningly behind the counter, obviously wondering where Phoebe was. 'Er, if you weren't expecting us, we could rearrange for another day,' she offered. 'We come to Brighton quite often in the summer.'

'No, it's fine,' Cerys said, mentally rearranging her afternoon. 'Phoebe will be home from preschool any minute. She does three afternoons with a childminder and I take a couple of afternoons off to be with her most weeks.' She chuckled. 'To be honest, half the time she goes for a nap and I end up back down in the shop with the baby monitor, but the thought's there on my part.' She smiled, ruefully. 'Working mother's guilt.'

'I don't want to interrupt her routine,' Jenny said, anxiously.

'Not at all,' Cerys assured her. 'When Phoebe hears there's a new friend to play with, a nap will be completely out of the question, believe me.' Despite her assurances, she hesitated, stealing a glance at her staff in the kitchen. Rico and Emma could probably manage without her for the extra hour, but – Cerys bit her lip, noting the flow of passers-by start to build up again on the street as people finished their lunches and returned to work or play – if there was a huge rush it could be tricky with just the two of them. Jenny saw her hesitation. 'It's really no trouble for us to come back another day, Cerys,' she said, no trace of offence in her expression.

'No,' Cerys insisted. 'You're not putting me out. I'll just have a quick word with my staff.' Even if she'd made the arrangement with Beth during a sleep-fuddled state, it had to be honoured one way or the other. And Jenny was going to be a friend, Cerys knew it.

Sitting at his desk at the central London office, Rich heard his phone vibrate in the desk drawer and pulled it out: MADE IT TO BRIGHTON. FOUND RISE. CERYS LOVELY, GIRLS ALREADY FRIENDS. THANKS. J XX

Rich grinned, delighted that the play date had worked out. Jenny had been on her own for several weeks now and he knew that Nathan was worried about her. 'Not that she can't cope,' he'd said in a hurried phone call to Rich a few nights ago. 'Heaven knows she's on her own with the kids most of the time as it is. But she's worrying about me and it's really getting to her. She needs something. I don't know. A distraction.' Hearing his friend's voice tight with anxiety and guilt, Rich had hurried to reassure him. 'I'm on it, mate. You concentrate on what you're doing out there. OK, is it?'

'Oh yeah, all quiet so far. There's the odd firecracker at night, you know how it is here. But nothing unusual.'

'Great. Well, leave it with me.'

'Thanks, Rich.'

It was one of the things Rich loved about their old friendship group. They might not see each other regularly, a fact Beth found astounding since they technically worked for the same company, albeit in completely separate departments and offices. The point was, with real friends, frequency of contact didn't matter. If you needed something, it would be done. It was his only true experience of family. Beth had come up with the idea of introducing Jenny to

Cerys and Phoebe. 'I know Jenny has loads of friends already, but it's a fresh face, a change of scenery,' she'd suggested as they'd pondered the problem over an al fresco supper in their back garden. 'And not too far on the train or by car.'

'Will they get on?'

'Oh, yes,' Beth had said with conviction. 'Cerys gets on with everyone.'

'So does Jenny.'

'No worries, then. I'll set it up.'

Rich jumped as his phone vibrated again in his hand. He smiled as Beth's name flashed up on the screen: STILL ON FOR TONIGHT? 7PM? XX

Quickly, he typed a reply: YEP, 7PM. DAVID PROM-ISES TO BE THERE XX

The reply came within seconds: HUH. BELIEVE IT WHEN I SEE IT. X

Rich chuckled and put the phone back in the drawer, out of his sight. If he got drawn into a long text conversation instead of reviewing the fine print of the contract in front of him, it would be him missing dinner, not David.

David stepped out of a black cab and waved his thanks to the driver as it crawled off into the heavy traffic. He felt like crawling off himself, preferably to somewhere in the shade with a large gin. Someone bumped into him, their briefcase catching his thigh as they hurried past, and David moved into the shadow of the nearest building. He felt hot and irritable, and thoroughly fed up with meetings. Reflected heat came off the building and rolled over him, a combination of over-used air mingled with traffic fumes. It moved in sluggish, semi-stagnant waves, ruffling his hair as it passed over him. How could you feel stifled and unable to breathe when there was a breeze? he thought, loosening his tie. Central London in August was not a good place to be. David thought long-ingly of all the places where there was a true breeze – bluff coastlines, rolling moorland, the Welsh mountains, and further afield, Cannes with its spectacular yachts, and Sicily.

'Damn it.' David pushed himself away from the wall. 'I'm going for a swim.' Pulling out his phone, he sent a vague email to his secretary before joining the stream of people rushing down the street. After three hours supporting the company's head of government relations in a meeting with the minister for the environment, he'd earned a couple of hours off. The company put a lot of resources into sustain-able energy and other so-called green projects, more than enough to offset the occasional hiccup here and there in the oil industry, in David's opinion. Despite his conviction, such men always managed to get under his skin, making him feel like an ethical outcast. However, with environmental con-cerns rapidly increasing in the public psyche, David was obliged to put in an appearance in support of their govern-ment relations officer at these 'discussions' from time to time. He picked up his pace, weaving through the slower pedes-trians, spurred on by the knowledge that a few vigorous lengths of butterfly stroke would thrash out his frustrations. There would still be plenty of time back in the office before dinner.

Fifteen minutes later, he was checking in at the health club where he and Carlotta had been members for years. The receptionist greeted him with a smile and handed him the key to his personal locker without asking for his name. David pulled out his swimming gear, making a mental note to bring two sets next time he came. Carlotta had always kept the locker stocked up so he could drop in unplanned if he felt like it. David tried to maintain the habit. The changing-room was quiet at this time of day, the lighting subtle and soothing, and the heated tile floor warming the soles of his feet. David lifted a white robe from a clothes rail and a towel from the neatly rolled selection pressed into open cubby holes beside the mirrors, enjoying the peace. Not many people were fortunate enough to be able to take time out mid-afternoon on a Wednesday, the turning point of the week. If you weren't on target by the end of Wednesday there'd be a cloud over you for the rest of the week, threatening your weekend.

David left the changing-room and sauntered towards the pool. It was a decent size, fifty metres long, with plenty of loungers and wicker tub chairs arranged singly and in groups on the periphery, tastefully divided and screened by large potted plants. A slatted wood sauna occupied the far end of the room, occasional steam escaping when the door opened, as if it were perpetually in a foul temper. David's face broke into a smile as he saw that the pool was deserted apart from a single swimmer at the far end, making lazy strokes through the water. He dumped his things on a lounger, tossed his locker key on top and plunged in with a crisp dive that barely rippled the surface. Five lengths later, he heaved himself onto the side and sat with his legs dangling in the water, breathing heavily. On the other side of the pool, the other swimmer backstroked towards the ladder. David watched as he got his breath back, wondering if his splashy stroke had caused offence. He shrugged. It was a free country, and he'd deliberately chosen the opposite side of the pool. The swimmer pulled herself up, water droplets clinging to her long limbs and athletic frame. She was wearing a red one-piece bathing suit and her hair was trapped in a loose bun at the nape of her neck. Something about the set of her shoulders made David look closer, and then she turned, shook her hair free and glanced up, suddenly aware of his scrutiny. David's breath caught in his throat. The train girl. Quickly he slid into the pool and dived into a glide, his pulse thudding in his ears.

Across the pool, Beth frowned. Strange Train Man? Surely not. She turned away, shrugging the idea off as swiftly as it had come. Middle-aged businessmen were ten a penny in this place, most of them good-looking. They all had a certain look about them. The silver clock on the wall showed plenty of time for a sauna, a leisurely shower and a cup of tea in the lounge before she had to meet Rich. By the time David surfaced, she was gone. Quickly, he climbed out of the pool, his mind made up. Once was coincidence. Twice was . . . he didn't believe in fate, but it was definitely more than coincidence. It had to be followed up. You're old. She's married. What exactly do you intend to say? He batted away the barrage of objections that came at him from all sides, driven on by the simple need to answer one question. Who was she?

Inside the sauna, Beth chose the seat furthest from the door and sat back with a sigh, her long legs folded beneath her. Someone had added menthol to the brazier and she breathed deeply, enjoying the intense heat. She closed her eyes. When the door creaked open, she kept them closed, willing the other person away. She had an evening of small talk ahead of her and had no intention of making polite chit-chat now. So she ignored the polite cough and the deliberate just-so-you-know-I'm-in-here-too shuffling and tried to clear her mind using a yoga meditation technique that her mother swore by. *I am light. I am light. My whole body is made up of light.*

Another cough. Beth ignored it. I am weightless, my spirit is spinning free.

'Baking in here, isn't it?'

I am at peace with myself, and with everything around me.

'Excuse me.'

I am light. I am light. I am light. Her teeth were gritted but she persisted. So did the man. 'Do you mind if I put more menthol on the coals?'

Beth gave up. *I am not light. I am hacked off.* 'Sure,' she said, getting up and moving towards the door. 'I was just leaving.' She realized with a slight shock that it was Train Man. What were the chances of that? He put out a hand to stop her, looking chagrined.

'Please, not on my account. I've disturbed you.'

'No, I was ready to go.'

'But you were so peaceful there,' he protested. 'I'll use the sauna later, after you've finished.' He stood up and Beth moved closer to the door. The man was creeping her out. More, there was something predatory in the way he was looking at her, sizing her up.

'I'm leaving now,' she repeated and slipped out, practically closing the door in his face. She left the pool area without looking back and showered quickly, plagued by the nagging thought that had come to her on the train platform.

She had seen this man before . . . somewhere. She almost knew him. Beth towelled her hair dry roughly, irritated and irritable. To run into a stranger twice in the space of a month, and in London – it almost amounted to stalking. Flicking her hair into a rough ponytail, she gave herself a quick once-over in the mirror. The delicate floral tea dress was crumpled but presentable and she looked fresh. 'Forget it,' she told her reflection and headed for the quiet lounge area, where she curled up with a drink and her book.

Half an hour later, Beth heard the polite cough. She raised her eyes slowly, an incredulous look on her face. There he was again, back in a business suit and hovering by her chair. Beth glared up at him. His tie was trailing from his jacket pocket, a ridiculous attempt to look casual, and there wasn't a hint of apology in his wide, brown eyes. Quite the opposite, in fact. He looked confident, eager. Beth slapped her book down on the coffee table, making the ice in her glass rattle. Enough was enough. 'I don't know what your problem is,' she said, angrily, 'but if you don't leave me alone *this minute* I'll have you thrown out.'

He smiled broadly, indicating the leather armchair beside her. 'I think we've got off on the wrong foot. May I?'

'No,' snapped Beth. 'And there *is* no foot to get off on, right or wrong.' She blushed, realizing how odd that sounded. 'Look, just go away, please. You're bothering me.' This was truer than she was prepared to admit. There was something about the burning intensity in those brown eyes . . .

David sat down, hands up in a placatory gesture as though calming a belligerent child. 'At least let me buy you a drink to apologize for disturbing your peace.'

'I'm married.'

He shrugged. 'Doesn't mean I can't apologize,' he said, leaning back in his chair to catch the barman's eye. Beth stood up and stuffed her book into her shoulder bag.

'Sorry, you're not my type.' *Charismatic, confident and good-looking? No, not my type at all.* She stamped on the traitorous thought, deliberately focusing on her left hand and her wedding ring.

David looked at her, his gaze candid. 'OK. The apology stands, with or without the drink.' He rose smoothly and moved away from her to back his statement up. Beth stared at him, caught between action and indecision.

'Have you been following me?'

'No.' He looked straight into her eyes without flinching. 'It's a very odd coincidence, bumping into you twice.' Beth hesitated. He did seem genuine, but . . . she shook her head.

'Look, no offence,' she said, hitching her bag onto her shoulder. 'But I don't want the drink, or the apology.' She flicked a glance at her watch. 'Or to bump into you again. Ever. Now I really do have to go. I've got an appointment.'

David nodded courteously and stood aside. 'Of course. Goodbye then, er . . . ?'

'Rebecca,' Beth lied.

'Rebecca.' The man looked as though he'd been handed a trophy. 'Goodbye, Rebecca. My apologies again.'

'Bye,' Beth muttered and hurried away. She knew without looking back that his eyes were following her, so she held her head high and lengthened her stride.

David waited until she had gone before gathering his own things. It wouldn't do to have her think he was following her again, however much he wanted to. He caught himself mouthing her name, trying it out, and gave himself a mental shake. 'You're ridiculous, man,' he said. 'And very nearly late.' He stepped onto the street and hailed a cab.

Rich was waiting outside the sushi bar when Beth rounded the corner at the end of the block, red-faced and puffing. 'Good job I wore flats,' she panted by way of greeting. 'Are we late?'

'Just a bit.' Rich kissed her and took her hand. 'Shall we go in?' Inside, the sushi bar was brightly lit and there was a cheerful buzz of noise. Although it was only just past seven, the place was already more than half full of hungry diners tucking into an early dinner. The tables closest to the door were set in a trestle style, the light wooden surfaces spotless and unfussy, individual flowers dotted here and there in contemporary white miniature vases. Further in were diner-style booths running down each wall, with padded leather seats in dark red. Beth looked admiringly at the walls, which held a mixture of framed Japanese scripts in bold, flowing black, and bright colour-block canvases in reds and purples. The overall effect was classy and cool without trying too hard. Beth felt instantly relaxed. 'We should have come here before,' she said to Rich above the noise. 'I like it.'

'Wait until you try the food,' he replied, smiling as a waiter approached them. 'It's awesome. Hi, table for Hampton, 7 o'clock. Sorry we're late.'

The waiter smiled, showing teeth even whiter than his high-collared shirt 'This way, sir. Your companion has already arrived.' He led them to a booth towards the back of the bar. 'Here we are.' Rich leaned down and pumped the hand of a handsome man in a crumpled business suit. 'Great to see you, mate,' he said, warmly. The man slid out of the booth and returned the handshake with a hug. Over Rich's shoulder, Beth's eyes met his and she froze. This was beyond a joke. Rich turned and laid his hand on her arm. 'David, this is Beth,' he said proudly. 'You meet at last.' He looked from one to the other. Beth was scarlet and David was doing his best not to laugh.

'*This* is David?' Beth spluttered.

'And this is Beth,' David grinned, stepping in to kiss her cheek. 'Not Rebecca.' Rich's face was a mask of confusion.

'Do . . . you two know each other?'

'No!' said Beth. 'Yes. Sort of.' Her thoughts were a whirl of confusion and guilt, though she knew she'd done nothing wrong.

'We've crossed paths,' David said, smoothly. He ushered Beth into the booth and flashed another smile at her. 'I'll let you explain, shall I? How about that drink?' Inside, he was torn between joy and despair. *Not just married, but Rich's wife.* It couldn't be worse. Or better, because here she was, right in front of him, and suddenly he felt alive again.

Chapter Seven

'Please, Jenny.'

'No.'

'Please.'

'Beth, I can't traipse the children all the way to a resort in Dubai for an Annual Bring-Your-Wife Strategy Weekend.' Jenny was apologetic but firm.

'They're paying for everyone to go first-class,' Beth cajoled her. 'And apparently there's a great pool. The kids would love it.'

'I'm sure they would,' Jenny said, wryly. 'I, however, would be ready for the men in white coats after half a day. Even if I wanted to go, it's just not possible.'

'But I'm begging you!' Beth knew she was whining, but desperate measures were needed.

'How can I put this?' Jenny mused, trying to keep the amusement from her voice. 'I have three children under 5, one of whom starts school in a few weeks. No is not a word I have difficulty with. Plus, I'm completely whine-proof.'

'You can't abandon me to *Them*.'

'It's really not that bad, Beth. And Rich will be there.'

'He won't! He won't! They work all day and most of the night.'

'You don't know that.'

'He told me,' Beth said, flatly.

'Really?' The surprise was evident in Jenny's voice. 'What an idiot. No wonder you don't want to go. Nathan told me it would be all sun, sea and cocktails the first time I went.'

Beth's voice brightened instantly. 'And was it?' She recoiled from the handset as Jenny roared with laughter.

'No, of course not. It was hideous. The men worked all day and then we had horribly drawn out formal dinners every night in the baking heat. The air-conditioning in our room was broken and I didn't sleep a wink. And, of course, I had to spend my days with . . . *Them*, as you put it.'

'But . . . but you said it wasn't that bad!' Beth wailed.

'On reflection, it's best you know from the outset,' Jenny said, frankly. 'Rich is right. At least this way you're prepared. Look, don't panic,' she went on as Beth started to gibber down the phone. 'You'll be OK. Some of them are very nice.'

'Who?'

'Beatrice Cecil.'

'Do-gooder.'

'Er . . . Jessica Nealson.'

'What, Barbie? The wife of the communications director? Come off it.'

'Er . . .' Jenny was almost out of ideas. 'Harriet Fothering-ham.'

'Housewife. Oh, sorry, Jenny,' Beth stuttered. 'I didn't mean – I mean, you were, you had . . .'

'I did have a career once, you mean?' Jenny chuckled. She'd been a journalist for Reuters before giving it up to start a family.

'How did you cope?' Beth asked, wretchedly.

'Cocktails, a stack of good books and a deep sense of gratitude,' Jenny replied, ticking them off on her fingers.

'Gratitude for what?'

'That I wasn't like them,' Jenny said. 'Cling to that, if nothing else.'

'They're a breed of their own, that's for sure,' Beth said, miserably. 'I just don't fit in.'

'Don't try,' Jenny advised. 'And,' she added, 'most importantly, make Rich promise not to invite you next year. Knowing it was a one-off made it much easier for me to bear. Do your duty once and then you can be busy for at least the next four years.' Beth heard a wail in the background.

'Do you have to go?' she asked.

'Hang on.' There was a pause while Jenny investigated. 'It's OK. Minor tricycle collision. No, Abi, don't hit him. It was an accident. Sorry, Beth. Where were we?'

'The depths of Stepford Wife despair,' Beth said, gloomily.

'Being overdramatic about it isn't going to help,' Jenny pointed out. 'Think of one good thing about the trip.'

'There isn't anything. Seriously. I'd rather crawl to the North Pole on my hands and knees,' Beth said, 'in a bikini.'

'You'll be supporting your husband.'

'Hmm. OK,' Beth admitted, grudgingly. 'I suppose that's a good thing.'

'Hold that thought,' Jenny ordered. 'Oh, hell.' Beth heard a faint crash.

'I'll let you go,' she said, swiftly. 'Thanks for the pep talk.'

'Any time. Abigail, *no!*' Jenny shouted, switching neatly between conversations in a way that would have hotwired

Beth's brain. 'Take care, Beth. Put him down. Down, I said. Bye, then. Talk soon.'

'Bye.' Beth shut her phone off and flopped down on the sofa like a rag doll. 'That's it, then,' she said, glumly. 'I'm on my own. Trapped between fake-tan airheads and knitting club members. Excellent.'

It was an odd thing about the wives of the great and the good in Rich's company. With a couple of notable exceptions, Jenny being the main one, there was no middle ground. On the one hand there were the faithful first wives, usually middle-aged, vigorous women who divided their time between charitable organizations and their children. Beth wasn't knocking them. Charities like Nightingale relied heavily on exactly that type of person. You just wouldn't want to spend three days in a row in close quarters with them.

Then, on the other hand, there were the second or third wives, usually much younger, who tended to be secretaries, personal assistants, or ladies of leisure. For some reason, the resultant social melting-pot produced toxic vapours every time. Beth herself was a kind of hybrid of the two groups, being in the younger age bracket but also Rich's first wife. She did volunteer for a charity and she was up to speed on children, thanks to Phoebe. Technically, she ought to tick all the boxes but . . . she just didn't fit. Her views were wrong, she was too bohemian, too much 'live and let live'. She had an independent career and lacked the competitive one-upmanship that ran like poison throughout the assembled wives. Beth had only attended a few dinners, but even those had deteriorated rapidly after the wine had gone round the table a couple of times. Conversations inevitably became competitive as each woman strove to justify themselves, and there were the inevitable sniping comparisons between children, holidays and, of course, the advancing careers of the beloved husbands. Before you knew it, the long knives were out and it was handbags at dawn. Beth's nature was too straightforward for that kind of environment, as was Jenny's.

'Three days,' she intoned, pronouncing it like a death sentence. 'Right.' She got up and plumped her stripy cushions in a bracing, get-over-yourself fashion. 'Enough.' It wasn't for a couple of weeks; she had time to prepare. Rich wholeheartedly supported her career, even when it meant short spells away, and this was the first time he'd asked her to accompany him. 'I won't have to go again,' she said, chanting it like a mantra as she absentmindedly threw the ingredients for a Victoria sandwich cake into a bowl and mixed feverishly. Beneath her dislike of the assembled Stepford Wives was a deeper spike of discomfort that she refused to acknowledge.

Cerys, on the other hand, went straight for the jugular with her usual accuracy when Beth rang her later that afternoon. 'Admit it, sis,' she said, pounding tomorrow's foccacia bread dough one-handed as she listened to Beth's tale of woe. 'It's Train Man.'

'What? Don't be stupid.'

'It is,' Cerys insisted. 'You're still sore about it.'

'In what way, Freud?' Beth scoffed, obviously not in the mood to be psychoanalyzed by Cerys, who knew her too well and was usually right.

'Simple.' Cerys flipped the dough and began kneading the other side, automatically checking for even distribution of the fresh rosemary throughout the mixture. Across the table, Phoebe copied the movement, little fingers pressing and kneading her own small piece of dough. Cerys wasn't teaching her to bake as such, but Phoebe was learning a lot just by watching. She was also listening intently to her mother's conversation, though apparently engrossed in her task. It couldn't be helped. 'He made you look like an idiot, and you're cross about it,' Cerys continued. 'Also,' she said, undeterred by Beth's derisive snort, 'you're cross because you misjudged him.'

'I did not misjudge him. I didn't know who he was.'

'You thought he was a weirdo, a stalker. Instead he turns out to be one of Rich's bosom buddies, pretty much his boss, *and* a really nice guy.'

'Well, he was alright,' Beth muttered.

'He was a good laugh, you said,' Cerys retorted. 'What was it again?' She frowned, trying to recall her sister's exact words: '*He was so easy to talk to, and funny. He makes you want to talk to him. I can see why Rich likes him so much.*'

'What are you, Rain Man?' Beth's voice sounded uncomfortable. 'I don't recall saying that, not exactly.'

'Mm. I do.' Cerys waited a second before delivering the killer blow. 'And he fancies you.'

'Cerys, that's enough,' snapped Beth.

'I'm only saying,' Cerys replied, calmly. 'Lots of men must fancy you. It doesn't mean there's a problem or anything.'

'Go and make bread and leave me be.'

'I am making bread. And *you* rang *me*.'

'Well, make more. And stop bugging me. You're as bad as Mum.'

'Oh, thanks a lot.'

Beth hung up and Cerys dropped her phone into her apron pocket, shaking her head.

'Is Aunty Beth having a bad day?' Phoebe piped up.

'No,' Cerys answered, smiling at her daughter's flour-smudged face. 'Sometimes Aunty Beth needs telling, and she doesn't like it. She won't be cross for long.'

Phoebe nodded solemnly. 'I don't like being told either,' she said. 'But sometimes mummies have to do the telling, don't they?'

'Yes, they do,' agreed Cerys.

Phoebe flipped her dough again and examined it closely, picking at a couple of herby specks. 'I expect she's gone to have a think in her room,' she said, sagely. 'She'll come out and say sorry in a bit, and you'll be friends again.'

'Oh, yes,' Cerys said reassuringly, hiding her smile. 'Aunty Beth never stays cross.'

Phoebe nodded importantly. 'That's alright then.' She held her dough out for inspection. 'I think mine's ready, Mummy. What do you think?'

Cerys moved closer to inspect her daughter's work, her chest suddenly tight with the realization that their first precious years were almost over. *I don't want you to go to school.* She threw her arms round the little girl and hugged her tight.

'Ow, Mummy!' Phoebe struggled in her grasp.

'Sorry, darling,' Cerys said, kissing her hair before letting go. 'I just love you so much.'

'I love you too, Mummy,' she replied, straightening her apron with dignity. 'But you're squashing my foccatchy dough.'

Cerys laughed. 'Come on, fusspot,' she said, lifting Phoebe off the stool. 'Let's bake it for Daddy. It can be part of his surprise dinner.'

'I can't wait for her to go to school,' Jenny sighed, settling onto the sofa with the phone on her lap. 'There, I've admitted it. What a horrible mother I am.' She kicked her shoes off and put her feet up on the coffee table. Her legs were throbbing after another day of charging around after Abigail and Michael. Beside her, Rory laughed, kicked his legs and stretched out a chubby hand to grasp the old-fashioned coiled cord connecting the phone and the receiver.

'You're a fantastic mother, Jenny,' Nathan said, loyally. 'Where are they now?'

'Upstairs, playing hide and seek in their pyjamas,' Jenny said, wearily. 'Don't worry, you know I wouldn't say it within earshot. Rory's chewing the phone wire if you want to say hello.'

'I'll have a quick word with them before I go,' Nathan replied, more concerned with the obvious fatigue in his wife's voice. 'How are you?'

'Fine. We've made a few trips down to Brighton to see Cerys and Phoebe. She did some baking with the girls on her day off last week, which Abigail loved. Rory's doing well, but he's got a tooth coming, so I think we're in for a few sleepless nights when you get back.' She yawned so widely that her jawbone clicked. 'Michael has discovered trees and keeps flinging himself at them. He can't climb them, nowhere near, but he's scraped his hands raw trying.'

'Poor little chap,' Nathan said. 'And Abi?'

'Full on, as ever.' There was no point in dissecting the various stand-offs and showdowns of the last few days. 'All the usual flashpoints. Shoes, pudding, outfit choices. She's bored, Nathan.' *And I'm exhausted.*

'School will soon fix that,' Nathan said. 'She's more than ready.' He hesitated. 'About this Strategy Weekend . . .'

'No,' Jenny said flatly.

'It would be a break for you,' Nathan said, apparently determined to persuade his wife. 'My mum has offered to have the children. We'd get a bit of time together.'

'I've already had this today from Beth Hampton,' Jenny said, suspiciously. 'Have you two been plotting?'

'Not at all. I just thought, you know, I'm flying straight there from Kazakhstan . . .'

'No, Nathan. It's a nice idea, but you know as well as I do that those weekends are horrendous. I'd rather wait the extra days until you come home properly.' Jenny pushed the phone aside and scooped Rory onto her lap as he started to grumble. 'Anyhow, I couldn't possibly leave Abigail so soon after she starts school. You know that. It's a big deal. I want to be there for her.' The line crackled as Nathan sighed heavily.

'You're right,' he admitted. 'I know you're right.' His voice lowered, making Jenny wonder where he was calling from. 'I miss you all so much.'

'I know, Nathan. We miss you too.' She felt tears threaten and forced an upbeat tone. 'It's not long now. How's it going out there?'

'Oh, OK, you know. The usual wrangling over the payments to the government, the exact location of the plant. You know what these contracts are like.' He was tired too, she could tell. 'We're nearly there now.'

'So they'll be sending the engineers out soon?'

'I hope so. Or they'll redeploy someone who's already out here . . . Enough shoptalk,' he said. 'It's depressing. Put the little man on and call the others.'

'OK. I love you, Nathan.'

'You too.'

'What do you mean, you're going to be late?' Cerys was aghast. 'You can't!'

'I'm sorry, love,' Martin replied, his voice tinny and distant on the hands-free set. 'It can't be helped. I've got to squeeze in another meeting.'

'But I had a nice dinner all planned,' she said. 'Phoebe's made foccacia bread.'

'You should have told me earlier,' he said, reasonably.

'Can't it wait?' Cerys pleaded. 'We haven't had dinner together all week.'

'No. It's a new client and they need some troubleshooting on their system. I'm really sorry.' Cerys didn't think Martin sounded terribly sorry, but she let it pass.

'I'll feed Phoebe and keep ours in the oven,' she offered. 'We can eat when you get home.'

'Thanks, but I'm probably going to be late. I'll pick up a burger or something on the way.'

'That's not a proper meal,' Cerys objected.

'Cerys, don't fuss.' Martin's tone told her his patience was wearing thin, but she was too cross to back down.

'Phoebe will be so disappointed.'

'That's not my fault, Cerys. You should have checked with me before building her up to it. I need some notice.'

'It was meant to be a surprise,' Cerys snapped, thinking of her stuffed vine leaves, and the sea bass all prepped and ready to be cooked. All for nothing.

'Cerys . . .'

'Forget it, Martin. Just forget it. You enjoy your burger.' She hung up and burst into tears. *Not so quick to psychoanalyze yourself, are you*, a traitorous voice whispered in her head. *Or your marriage*. 'Oh, shut up,' Cerys sniffed, and went in search of some dough to pound.

Chapter Eight

Beth was in the shed. It was only a shed on the outside, but the thought of stepping into the garden with a cheery wave and saying, 'Just popping down to the dark room,' was way too pompous. There'd been a brief period when Rich had dubbed it the Black Hole, but the name hadn't stuck.

'If you've got the shed, where am I going to go when I want to sulk?' he'd enquired when he first moved into the cottage. Beth had presented the cupboard under the stairs with a triumphant flourish and granted him permanent rights to it on the spot, provided he was willing to share with the hoover.

Though she never used the traditional developing method professionally, it was something she enjoyed messing about with in her own time. Going through the process manually created a great sense of purpose, and Beth found it very peaceful. You had to be fully present to what you were doing, so that any other thoughts or worries were sloughed away and your mind was left clear and focused on the job in hand. This batch of photos was of Phoebe, taken last time she'd come to visit. Beth had watched her pottering about the garden, interrogating Rich about the various plants and shrubs, and had snatched up her camera. Children of Phoebe's age were the perfect subjects – old enough to be interesting and engaging, but young enough not to have developed the 'pose and smile' reflex that became ingrained in so many people.

Beth looked at one of the newly developed shots. It was still drying, but the picture was clear enough. If Beth squinted at the photo, it wasn't Phoebe grinning back at her but Cerys, the big brown eyes gazing straight up at her. Reproachfully. Turning her back on the photo, Beth opened the door a crack, just enough to allow her to shimmy out without exposing her precious shots. She was still sore about her sister's comments. Beth knew it was childish, but hadn't been taking Cerys's calls for the last couple of days. This was a sure sign that her comments had hit the mark. Beth knew this as well. She also knew, with a growing sense of unease, that she didn't want to see David again. This made no sense. Beth wandered down the garden and plucked the head of a dying rose from the trellis on their patio. She pulled the petals off one by one, naming every argument she could muster against this irrational feeling.

One: He was an old friend of Rich's and therefore deserved her courtesy and respect.

Two: However rarely he turned up to social events, he was a part of Rich's social and professional circles and would ultimately be impossible to avoid.

Three: He didn't appear to be a man to hold a grudge, and had been amused rather than offended by her behaviour towards him before their formal introduction. Beth winced at the memory of their conversation in the health club bar, when she had all but accused him of being a stalker.

Four: David was a nice man – good company, engaging and, as Cerys had reminded her, easy to be around.

Beth frowned, her thoughts scattering like the falling petals. Why did she feel uneasy about him? Her mind produced a snapshot memory, an image of David watching her through the carriage window of the train at Waterloo. From the platform she had felt his gaze on her, turned back and seen ... Beth screwed her eyes up, trying to re-enter the moment ... there had been an intensity to his gaze, as though he was committing her face to memory, down to the tiniest detail. With a jolt, she placed the expression. It was exactly how Rich looked at her when he left for a business trip, only somehow hungrier. To have a stranger look at you that way was ... Beth shrugged, at a loss. Weird? Unnatural? Slightly freaky? 'All of those,' she decided. But not unpleasant. She turned towards the setting sun, narrowing her eyes to take in the red-gold of the dying day. Undoubtedly she was reading too much into it. Tendrils of doubt curled about her mind, and she brushed them away.

Behind her, the back door opened and Rich popped his head out. 'Ready for supper, beautiful?' he grinned, brandishing two plastic carrier bags. 'I picked up a takeaway on my way home.'

Beth's eyes lit up. 'Indian?'

'Yep.'

'Great.' She followed him in, crushing the discarded petals underfoot.

Later on, as Beth was tidying up the debris from their meal, Rich disappeared upstairs and returned with a tatty leather-bound photo album. 'Got something to show you here,' he announced, laying it carefully on the kitchen table.

'Oh yes?' Beth dried her hands on a chequered tea towel and pulled a chair up beside him.

'Yeah. Since we'll all be together on the Strategy Weekend, I thought you might like to see a cool shot of the old gang in the glory days,' he grinned, referring to his university years. 'See how kind the years have been. Let's see . . .' Rich began leafing rapidly through the album, pushing loose pictures aside as he went.

'Hold on, you're going too fast,' Beth protested.

'No, it's a particular photo I'm after,' he said, mock-slapping her hand away. 'You've seen most of these before anyway. Patience.' Beth bit her tongue and waited. 'Ah.' Rich slowed down and began looking at the pages more carefully. 'It should be somewhere about . . . here.' He nudged the album closer to Beth and tapped a faded print. Beth leaned in, recognition sparking in her eyes.

'That's it!' she exclaimed, jabbing a finger at the picture. 'You had a print of this in a frame, didn't you?'

'Er . . .'

'You did,' she insisted. 'At your old house. It was in the loo.'

'You mean that old collage of university photos?' He looked disappointed that she'd seen it before. 'I didn't realize this picture was in with that.'

'Yes.' Beth felt an overwhelming sense of relief. 'And *that's* where I knew him from.' She wasn't going mad after all.

'Knew who?' Rich looked completely at sea.

'David. When I saw him that day on the train, I knew I had seen him somewhere before, I just knew it.' She slid the photo out of its protective plastic film and held it up to the light. 'Thought I was losing the plot for a bit, but here's the proof. I was right.' Four men – boys, really – lined up on a

riverbank with their arms across each other's shoulders. They
were wearing matching white shorts and T-shirts, and wore
identical expressions of exhilaration and laughter, presum-
ably after a rowing victory against a rival college.

'You and your photographic memory,' Rich said fondly,
kissing the bare skin on her shoulder.

'David, Nathan, you . . .' Beth moved her finger slowly
over the photo, coming to a stop by the fourth boy, a blond
brandishing an oar. 'But who's this?'

'That's Jonathan,' Rich said. Beth looked up sharply,
catching the sober note in his voice.

'You've never mentioned him,' Beth said softly, wondering why.

'No?' Rich scuffed a hand through his hair, his eyes sad.
'Well, it's a long time ago now. We were all close, but he was
David's friend first. His best friend. David and Jonathan came
as a package deal, so he was part of our crowd. They'd been
at prep school together and were pretty much joined at the
hip, even when Carlotta came on the scene. Jonathan was a
real joker. We had some great times.' Beth studied the photo
more closely and saw that David and Jonathan, positioned at
opposite ends of the photo, were grinning not at the camera
but at each other, as though sharing a secret joke.

'Where is he now?' she asked.

'He died,' Rich replied. 'Not long after we graduated,
actually.'

'Oh. How?'

'Ambiguous circumstances,' Rich said gruffly, plucking
the photo from Beth's fingers. 'Never resolved.' He closed the
album and stood up, his body communicating an unvoiced

but extreme discomfort with the line of conversation. 'Like I said, a long time ago now.' He set the album aside with a finality that warned Beth not to pursue her questions further. *Why show me if you didn't want to talk about it?* she thought, surprised at this hidden corner of Rich's history and his reluctance to discuss it. It told her one thing for certain – Rich must have been very attached to Jonathan. The only things he ever shied away from discussing were emotive topics, particularly sad ones. Aloud she said, 'Cup of tea?' and smiled as his face brightened instantly.

'I'll make it,' he offered, his sunny nature quick to reassert itself as always. 'You'd better think about packing.'

'I'm on it,' Beth answered with a salute. She turned away before the smile fell off her face, tugging her good mood with it. Three days, she reminded herself. The photo flashed up, young David's head turning across the shot, his eyes piercing the photographic paper to reach hers. Even portrayed remotely, his charisma was astonishing. 'God help me.' The phrase came automatically, but Beth was alarmed to discover that for the first time in her life, she actually meant it.

Predictably, Dubai was hot. Also predictably, Beth was foaming at the mouth within hours of arrival and had nearly bitten her tongue clean through with the effort of maintaining a semblance of good manners. Unwilling to engage with the constant verbal swordplay of the other wives, she adopted fugitive tactics, hiding out wherever there was a power point for her laptop, and attempting to move around the hotel on a different schedule to the rest of the group. When confronted, she pleaded work as her excuse.

'But you're a photographer,' objected Harriet Fothering-ham, her Gucci shades wobbling on their precarious perch atop her bleached blonde hair. She had spotted Beth in the far corner of the lounge bar and homed in on her with the intention of persuading her to join the group by the hotel pool. Beth knew full well there would be another agenda behind the kind request. There always was with these women.

'That's right, I am,' Beth agreed as politely as she could, dropping her eyes immediately back to her work. Harriet remained where she was, her pointed stare demanding further explanation; after all, how could there possibly be anything more important than gossiping by the pool with the other ladies? Beth stared at her laptop screen with equal determina-tion, biting the inside of her cheek to keep from laughing. After a minute or so she raised her head. 'I wouldn't dream of keeping you,' she said, sweetly. 'It's beautiful outside.' Rich would tell her off later for making waves, but she didn't care.

'I see,' replied Harriet, frostily. 'No doubt we'll see you at dinner, if your work permits.' She flounced away, flip-flops slapping furiously on the tiled floor. Once she was well out of sight Beth pushed her laptop aside, sat back and stretched, enjoying the peace. The lounge bar was beautifully decorat-ed, its plain walls offsetting the soft furnishings and thick, patterned rugs, their colours a mixture of rich reds and golds. Overhead, broad propellers revolved on electric fans, the gentle whirring blending into calming white noise. Beth squinted at the one closest to her, attempting to count the number of propellers. The effort hurt her eyes.

'Penny for your thoughts?'

David was suddenly beside her, fresh and relaxed in light linen trousers and a short-sleeved shirt. Beth hadn't heard him approach.

'Where did you spring from?' she asked.

'The dark depths of a meeting room,' he grinned, dropping into a chair beside her. 'But you seem to be having your own private meeting here.'

'Oh . . .' Beth clicked her work off the screen. 'Not really. Just some work for a charity I'm involved with.' She glanced at the double doors that led to the body of the hotel. 'Is Rich coming out too?'

David's face momentarily darkened, no more than a brief tightening around the eyes, swiftly replaced by his usual easy smile, but Beth noticed it. 'Yes, he'll be along in a minute,' he replied, sitting back and stretching his legs out, revealing ankles that were milk-bottle white. 'You haven't answered my question yet.'

'Huh?'

'Your thoughts,' he said. 'Penny for them.'

Beth arched her eyebrows. 'Nothing in particular,' she hedged. 'A bit of charity work.'

'Ah yes, Rich told me,' David said, moving the conversation smoothly on. 'Nightingale. What's your involvement?'

'Just a few publicity shots now and again,' Beth lied, unwilling to seem as though she was showing off.

'That's not what Rich says.'

'Then he's exaggerating.'

David sat forward, elbows resting on his knees, and Beth immediately leaned back, instinctively increasing the distance between them. His gaze made her uncomfortable.

'Seriously, Beth,' he said, and her skin prickled at the sound of her name in his mouth. 'You shouldn't hide your light under a bushel.'

'I've never heard anybody use that expression, apart from my mother and the vicar.'

'It is old-fashioned,' he agreed, frowning as a thought struck him. 'What does a bushel look like anyway? Have you ever seen one?'

'Only from the inside,' Beth answered without missing a beat. David threw back his head and laughed. 'You're too smart for me,' he admitted. 'I'll leave you in peace.' He stood up to leave, then turned back on a whim. 'Unless . . .'

'What?'

'You don't fancy a swim before dinner, do you? Not the main pool,' he went on, seeing the impending refusal in Beth's eyes. 'There's another one up on the roof. Not many people seem to know it's there.' Beth stared incredulously at him. Was he propositioning her? 'We could drag Rich out of his meeting,' David added, almost as an afterthought. 'He's due a break.'

'Thanks, but I'll wait for him here,' Beth said, coolly.

'No problem. Don't work too hard,' he said, with a nod at the laptop. 'Enjoy the rest of your afternoon.'

David walked away, cursing himself for his clumsiness. He'd overstepped the mark and he knew it. He felt a stab of guilt, knowing that had she accepted, he wouldn't have hesitated. Just to spend some time with her, he argued. Nothing else.

Beth watched him go, her heart thumping. 'You're imagining things,' she told herself firmly. 'Get a grip.' But deep down she knew that for a fraction of a second, part of her had been tempted to accept. Her heart skipped a beat. For all the sickness of guilt she felt inside, there was more than a hint of excitement. *He's an attractive man, Beth. You're just feeling flattered. That's all. Any normal woman would.* But as she tried to dismiss the thought of him from her mind, she was more than disturbed to find it wasn't easy.

They retired early that night, Beth prising Rich away from the bar, where he was deep in conversation with Nathan. 'Sorry, Nathan,' she smiled. 'I've had enough for one night.'

He glanced over his shoulder at the gaggle of women draped over the sofas, and grinned back at her. 'Can't say I blame you,' he said. 'Jen would be hot on your heels if she were here.'

'I wish she was.'

'Me too,' sighed Nathan. He slid off his bar stool and clapped Rich on the shoulder.

'In fact, I think I'll go and call her now.'

'She'll still be up?' Beth asked, surprised.

'She doesn't sleep too well when I'm away,' Nathan replied.

Rich shot Beth a look that warned her to say no more. 'Night, mate,' he said, leading Beth away.

They were both tired and wasted no time getting into bed, where they lay face to face, the sheet drawn up against the chill of the air-conditioning which was jammed on the highest setting.

'Are they being dreadful to you?' Rich asked, stroking her cheek with the back of his hand.

'Only because I won't play,' Beth answered with a shrug.

'Well, I wish you would,' he said, his smile taking the sting from his words. 'They were all over me at dinner, it was horrendous. One of them was actually clutching my sleeve.'

'Funny, wasn't it?'

'Typical, more like,' he said, mournfully. 'All these years I wait for a wife of my own to protect me from all the others, and I get one who doesn't care.'

'You don't need protection,' she laughed, rolling onto him and locking her arms about his neck. 'And anyway, I do care. Just not about them.' She lay awake for a long time after Rich fell asleep, watching the even rise and fall of his chest. He could be stuck in a tent halfway up a mountain in a hurricane and still he would sleep like a log. The sleep of the just, her mother called it. Beth wasn't so lucky. After an hour of tossing and turning she slipped out of bed, grabbed her swimming things and left the room. She didn't know how to get to the rooftop pool David had spoken of, but it was worth a try. If nothing else, a quick walk about might clear her head and help her sleep.

At the end of the corridor she paused by the lift, but decided to take the stairs. Seconds later the lift doors slid open and David caught a glimpse of her as she disappeared around the corner. Seeing the towel trailing from her arm, he guessed her intention and followed unsteadily, his brain addled from alcohol and fatigue. He had just enough wit to remain out of sight, loitering in the final stairwell until he heard the outer door swing closed above him. He waited there for what felt like an eternity, doing battle with himself. After some time, he mounted the remaining steps slowly, and though his feet dragged with every step, the compulsion was too strong to resist.

There was a small window set into the door. David leaned heavily against the wall, positioned so that he could see without being seen. It was dark in the pool, but solar lights gave out the sun's remembered glow, casting enough light for him to make out Beth's silhouette. She dived lightly into the pool and began to swim, her limbs fluid and graceful as she moved through the water. When she climbed out, her hair slicked back and her body gleaming with a thousand water droplets, like tiny jewels all over her body, David's conscience gave up the fight. *I want her. No matter what.* As he stumbled away down the stairs, the words settled deep within him and slowly began to spread, like a viper's bite.

Chapter Nine

'Good gracious, Elizabeth, what on earth's happened to you?'

'Er . . .' Beth glanced down at herself, wondering whether she'd put her clothes on inside out or stood in something she shouldn't have. They were in Kensington on what Cerys called one of their mother's 'Crock of Gold trips'. These tended to be spur of the moment purchases prompted by her current hobby.

'This!' her mother said, seizing Beth's arm and shaking it. She gave a squawk of fright and pulled away as though she'd found an unexploded grenade and discovered Beth's arm was the pin. 'It's not measles is it?' she hissed in a dramatic whisper. 'Only I was never vaccinated against it, you see, after an aunt of mine had the injection and went blind.' She pursed her lips reflectively, batting her paisley silk scarf off her face as it fluttered in the October wind, catching in her long silver-grey hair. 'Actually, I think it was the cataracts that caused the blindness, but Aunt Margaret always held that it was the vaccination, so of course Mummy wouldn't let us anywhere near it. It isn't, is it?' she finished, breathlessly.

'Isn't what?' Beth took a few moments to piece together the sense of this garbled outburst, her attention mainly on the road they were waiting to cross. Health matters formed the basis of a huge contradiction in her mother's nature. Beryl

Springfield would happily take on a bank robber armed with nothing more than righteous indignation and a handbag, but if you threatened her with so much as a common cold she could reach a state of hysteria in under twenty seconds. On the other hand, she was rock solid in her belief that a dab of holy water did you infinitely more good than anything modern medicine might prescribe.

'Are you sure it's not *measles*, darling?' her mother repeated, looking furtively around as though the surrounding pedestrians might hear her and flee from the oncoming pestilence.

'Oh.' Beth saw a gap in the traffic and stepped out onto the zebra crossing, chivvying her mother along. She looked down at her arm, still liberally sprinkled with raised red bumps after the trip to Dubai. 'No. Mosquito bites.'

'How did you get those?'

'Night swimming,' Beth answered shortly, one eye on her watch and the other on the clouds gathering overhead. Neither of them had an umbrella and Beth had dashed out in a short-sleeved shirt without so much as a cardigan to cover her arms. That was the trouble when the seasons turned, she mused, grasping her mother's elbow and picking up the pace. It took a while for you to switch to the appropriate weather accessories and clothes. In her case, it usually meant getting burnt, frozen or drenched once or twice before she remembered.

'You mean your repellent wasn't waterproof?' her mother tutted, forcing Beth's attention back to their conversation.

'Clearly not,' Beth said, dryly.

'Really, darling, did I teach you nothing about health risks when travelling abroad?'

Beth rolled her eyes helplessly. This was a bit much coming from the woman who had once hitchhiked round Europe for three months with nothing but a rucksack, a multilingual phrase book and a smile. Still, she held her tongue.

'You are feeling alright, though, aren't you?' her mother continued, peering anxiously into her face. Beth couldn't resist.

'Well, the bites are taking a long time to heal, and I have been feeling a bit feverish the last couple of days,' she admitted, regretting the joke instantly as terror sparked in her mother's eyes.

'Oh, help! Oh!' She gripped and dropped Beth's arm reflexively as her brain apparently tried to calculate the possibility of contagion. 'It's malaria, isn't it? You've got malaria. You need medication. What can we do?'

'Stop,' Beth said firmly, planting herself in front of her mother and causing an instant pile-up on the pavement before the following pedestrians adjusted their course, flowing round to either side of them. 'It's not malaria.' She gripped her mother's hands to prevent her from wringing them. 'I was winding you up, Mum. I'm sorry.'

Beryl sagged with relief before whipping her hands away and whacking Beth hard with her handbag.

'What was that?' Beth yelped, skipping quickly out of range. 'The latest alternative treatment?'

'If you like,' her mother sniffed, taking Beth's arm and striding out along the road to cover her embarrassment. 'And there's plenty more where that came from. Feverish indeed. You shouldn't do that to me, darling. It gave me a real turn.'

'Sorry,' Beth said dutifully, her grin contradicting the apology. 'I won't do it again.'

'You're as bad as your father was,' Beryl muttered crossly, though her answering smile told Beth she was off the hook. Beth put her arm round her mother's shoulders and gave her a comforting squeeze, always aware that nothing could really fill the hole left by her father's death three years ago. Beth and Cerys did their best, and Beryl's relationship with Phoebe had provided enormous comfort. Her insatiable appetite for hobbies and night classes did the rest. Beth often felt they were plugging the gap with hundreds of little pieces, like a mosaic, when what was really needed was one perfectly shaped piece – preferably person-shaped. Her mother flatly refused to consider another relationship, even on the basis of companionship. 'One marriage, one man,' she said, stubbornly. 'That's enough for me.' Beth maintained the hope that Beryl would change her mind, though Cerys regularly told her to forget it.

'Here we are,' Beryl said brightly, the mini-drama already forgotten. She tugged Beth onto a side street and headed towards a white-fronted shop, its window filled with colourful ceramic pieces mounted on clear Perspex blocks. To Beth the arrangement looked like Lego for grown-ups. 'This is where my pottery teacher works in the daytime,' Beryl explained. 'I'm after one of her abstract pieces, you'll love it. "Persephone's Garden", it's called.'

'Great,' said Beth, giving her best impersonation of enthusiasm. 'I haven't got long though, Mum.' Her brain flicked through the endless To Do list. There were some photos that needed submitting for a magazine feature and she wasn't yet happy with the editing she'd done, there were some calls to make and an invoice that needed chasing . . .

'Elizabeth?'

'Hmm?' Beth realized she'd come to a standstill in the street, staring blankly at the ground.

'Come on, then, if you're in a rush,' her mother said impatiently, beckoning her into the shop. 'I want you to meet Anoushka.' Squaring her shoulders, Beth followed her over the threshold, vainly hoping the place was more reasonably priced than it looked.

Not many miles away, Rich was having similar thoughts as he eyed the restaurant David had chosen. He had no objections to paying out for a nice dinner, but it seemed rather wasteful to push the boat out for a snatched lunch meeting. It would go on company expenses in any case, but the point remained. Rich took a deep breath before pushing through the double-fronted doors, already trying to second-guess the reason for the meeting. He found David already in place at the table. His head was bent over the wine menu, apparently oblivious to the neatly dressed sommelier hovering by his side, but he looked up as soon as Rich approached, his face breaking into a smile. 'Glad you could make it,' he said, warmly.

'Sorry I'm late,' Rich replied. He waited until David had ordered the wine before cutting to the point. 'What's the occasion?' he asked without preamble. David laughed, not offended by his friend's bluntness.

'We haven't even ordered food yet,' he said. 'There's no need to get straight down to business.'

'But this isn't regular business,' Rich replied, shaking the starched white napkin out and settling it on his lap. 'Our paths barely cross at work in the day-to-day run of things. What's so important that it merits all this?' His gesture took in the entire room, from the elegantly coiffed ladies at the adjacent table to the waiting staff gliding discreetly among the smartly dressed diners. The staff moved so smoothly Rich had the ridiculous notion that if he yanked up a passing trouser leg he might find they were all on roller skates.

'Business lunch,' David said.

'We could have met at head office.'

'OK, you've got me,' David sighed, holding his hands up. He should have known that trying to soften Rich up was a pointless exercise. He was too straightforward to be at all affected by that kind of persuasion tactic. There was nothing for it but to plunge straight in. 'I need a favour.'

'Pretty big favour,' Rich said mildly, eyeing up the cost of the steak on the menu.

'Yes,' David said, frankly. 'I'm afraid it is.' Rich's heart sank. He closed the menu and laid it on the table to attract the waiter's attention.

'It's Kazakhstan, isn't it?' he said quietly, reading the answer in his friend's face. 'The redeployment Nathan spoke of at the Strategy Weekend. You want me to oversee the new gas field in Karachaganak.'

'Yes.'

'How long?'

'Maybe a few months,' David said, tentatively.

'There are plenty of people you could send out there,' Rich pointed out. It was highly unusual for a director to be sent away for a long period; unprecedented, in fact.

'I can't trust anyone else with the job,' David offered by way of mitigation. 'The situation out there is somewhat delicate at present, as you know from Nathan's input at the Strategy Weekend.'

'Is that supposed to make me feel better about it?' Rich grunted. 'Anyhow, there's no way I can do that and cover my bases here as well. It's not practical.'

'We can move someone across to cover you in the interim,' David said casually, taking a brief sip of the wine and nodding at the sommelier to pour. 'I've worked it all out.'

'I can see that.' Rich drank deeply from his glass, but the red wine tasted of celebration and he took no pleasure from it. David leaned forward, desperate to close the deal. He needed to push this through.

'Please, Rich. Your technical expertise is unparalleled. We need you out there. You can take an apartment in Aktobe and commute.' He paused, gauging his friend's reaction. 'Will you do it for me?'

Rich sighed. 'When you put it like that, do I really have a choice?' he asked.

'There's always a choice,' said David softly, flinching inwardly as his words turned back on him, their truth cutting at his conscience. Rich said nothing for a while, but sat toying with his cutlery, watching the play of light down the length of his knife if he tilted it just so. David's fingers crumbled a corner of his bread roll, the action betraying his nerves, had Rich been alert enough to see it. As it was, all Rich could see was Beth's face, picturing the tears in her eyes when he told her, and the strength she would summon to keep them from spilling over in his presence. She'd turn away from him, put the kettle on and fetch him a huge piece of cake, chatting brightly about what he should pack and where he'd be staying. But if he woke in the night and reached out, he would find her pillow wet with tears. Rich let the knife slip from his fingers, the serrated edge grinning up at him like a row of silver teeth. There and then he resolved to get out.

'I'll do it,' he said, hating himself for agreeing to it. David's face broke into a smile. He reached out and grasped his friend's hand across the table.

'You're a good man,' he said, relief or guilt making him unusually emotional. 'And listen,' he went on earnestly, motioning at a waiter to take their order, 'don't worry about Beth. Now that we've met a few times, I hope she'll be comfortable enough to call on me for anything she needs.' He struggled to keep his tone light and diffident, though inside he was singing. 'I can look out for her while you're gone.'

'I'd appreciate that,' Rich said, gratefully. 'You're a good friend, David.' David smiled back at him, swallowing the disgust that rose up like bile in his throat. *I can't help it. I can't.*

'Darling, I can't help it.'

'You could have said no.' Rich tried to take Beth's hand but she pulled away from him and left the room.

'Beth, wait.' Panicking, he sprang off the sofa and followed her into the kitchen, catching her round the waist as she dumped the dinner plates into the sink and attacked them with a cloth. She was taking the news much harder than he'd imagined. Beth carried on with the washing-up, but neither did she shrug him off. Taking this as a good sign, Rich ploughed on. 'I know it's potentially for longer than usual, but . . .' he broke off as Beth muttered something. 'Sorry?'

'I said it's not potentially longer, it is longer,' she snapped.

'Alright, fair enough, but I –'

'A few months, you said. You've never been away for more than a few weeks up to now.'

'I know,' he said, desperately trying to placate her. 'But I'll probably be able to come back once or twice for a weekend.' Beth maintained a stony silence, but Rich thought he felt her relax against him. He kissed her hair, inhaling the scent of her shampoo. 'I hate it as much as you do,' he said.

'Then don't go.'

'This is the last trip,' he announced, playing his trump card. 'And then I'll look for another position, or . . . or get something written into my contract so that I don't have to go away any more.' Beth half-turned in his arms.

'Do you really mean that?'

'100 per cent.' He smiled down at her. 'We could start a family then. If you're ready, that is,' he added, as her eyes filled with tears.

'I'd like that.' Rich pulled her close, resting his cheek against the crown of her head. 'It doesn't mean I'm OK with the trip, though,' she said, her voice muffled by his shirt.

'I know.' Rich was wise enough not to push his luck. Beth pulled back so she could see his face. 'Was this Nathan's idea?' she asked, suspiciously. 'He was in Kazakhstan before you.'

'No,' Rich grinned. 'Don't add him to your hit list.'

'He knows you're going, though?'

'Yes. It wasn't his decision, but apparently he fully agreed with the proposal.'

'Some friend he is,' Beth said grumpily, and went in search of the cake tin.

'I couldn't have disagreed more,' Nathan said, staring moodily into his gin and tonic. Jenny was buzzing around the kitchen, loading washing, stacking plates and gathering items for Abigail's packed lunch.

'Then you should have spoken up, Nathan,' she said, distractedly.

'I did,' he protested. 'Repeatedly, and in the most strenuous terms. David was having none of it.' He frowned as he recalled the conversation. 'There are at least two other staff engineers experienced enough to do the job, and I know for a fact that one of them is coming to the end of a project any time now, so he'd be available to go.' The ice cubes in his glass clinked as Nathan swirled the liquid round, as though hoping to see answers floating amid the bubbles in his tonic. 'It makes no sense to send Rich out there; none at all.'

'Hang on a second, I'm still listening.' Jenny dived into the utility room and reappeared with her arms full of static-charged clothes from the tumble dryer. 'And you said all this to David?' she asked, dumping them on the table and sifting through the pile for socks to pair up.

'Virtually word for word,' Nathan replied, spotting an unmatched pair and automatically joining in. They worked in silence, the mindlessness of the task calming Nathan's frazzled nerves.

'It does seem odd,' Jenny said after a while.

'It's more than odd, it's irrational,' Nathan said, switching from socks to babygros. 'Something's wrong, Jen.' He bit his lip, unable to adequately voice his sense of foreboding. 'Rich won't want to leave Beth, I know that much.' Jenny tossed the last pair of socks onto the pile and gave him a hard look.

'You've got one of your feelings, haven't you?'

'I think so,' he admitted. 'I can't put my finger on it, but there's something bad in all this. Nothing about it fits, and the whole thing feels forced.' He shook his head. 'I'm rambling.'

'You should pray about it,' Jenny said, seriously.

'I think I will.' Nathan drained his drink and dragged himself to his feet. 'Let's go to bed. It'll all look clearer in the morning.'

Jenny nodded. 'Here, take these.'

'I feel like a clothes horse,' he complained, his chin just clearing the folded washing she dumped in his outstretched arms.

'I prefer laundry mule,' she grinned, scooping up a second load and heading for the stairs. 'Trot on, Dobbin.'

Chapter Ten

'You will come, won't you, Mummy?' Phoebe said anxiously, her dark eyes fixed on her mother's face. Her breakfast sat untouched, even her beloved chocolate bread forgotten. 'You will be there?'

'I'll be there,' Cerys said solemnly, busy assembling the various components of Phoebe's packed lunch. After a term of school, the list was deeply embedded in Cerys's subconscious. Ham sandwich, yoghurt, chopped pineapple and mango, fruit juice, a little tub of olives and a piece of cheese. Though eclectic in composition, it had to be the same every day, though Cerys was occasionally permitted to alter the type of bread. Any stealthy attempts at further variations were returned uneaten.

'And you won't be late?' Phoebe pressed. Cerys zipped up the treasured Pink Fairy lunchbox and set it on the table with a smile.

'I promise I won't be late,' she said. 'Cross my heart and hope to die.'

'Stick a needle in your eye?'

'Well, I don't know about –'

'Mum-*eeee*!' Phoebe's eyes filled with tears.

'Alright, OK,' Cerys said, hastily. 'Stick a needle in my eye.' Phoebe smiled and picked up her chocolate bread with its thick coating of butter and raspberry jam, then dropped it back on her plate as a second worry presented itself.

'And Daddy?'

'He'll be there too,' Cerys assured her, hoping Phoebe wouldn't extract another needle-jabbing promise from her. There were no guarantees on that score. Martin was working further and further afield lately, often leaving before dawn and not returning until midnight or beyond. He had promised to be there, but . . . Cerys shrugged the thought away, feeling disloyal. 'Don't worry, darling.' After eyeing Cerys warily for a second, Phoebe gave a satisfied nod and finally tucked into her breakfast.

'I'm just saying it, Mummy,' she said, spraying crumbs all over her uniform, 'because the angel Gabriel is only on at the beginning and a bit in the middle. I don't want you to miss the part where we frighten the shepherds.'

'That's the bit I'm most looking forward to,' Cerys replied, turning away to hide the tears that sprang to her eyes. She resolved to call Martin as soon as Phoebe was safely out of the way at school. Surely he wasn't going to miss their daughter's first school play. He had said that he would try, hadn't he? Cerys's memory kicked in, replaying their mumbled conversation in the pre-dawn gloom of the bedroom.

'I'll be there if I can,' Martin had said; that was it. But he'd had his back to her, bending over to pull his socks on, and so she hadn't been able to see his face. Cerys bit her lip, working her way around the kitchen on autopilot as her brain raced through the worst case scenarios. Martin lost, Phoebe hysterical with tears on stage, and forgetting her lines/Martin late, Phoebe equally hysterical/Martin just . . . not turning up/Phoebe hysterical. Cerys looked down and realized she was gripping the edge of the sink with both hands so hard that her knuckles had gone white. 'Calm down,' she told herself. 'He said he'd try.' *But that's not the same as saying he'll be there.* Worst of all, she knew that if Martin didn't show up, Phoebe, with her rigid 4-year-old view that mothers are in charge of The Whole World, would blame her. Cerys murmured a prayer and made an effort to shunt all negative thoughts into an unused corner of her mind, like out-of-service train carriages in a siding. She stretched a wide smile over her face and hoped it was broad enough to mask her worry. Phoebe was now driving the remaining sliver of chocolate bread around on her plate, making crushing noises as she ran over stray crumbs.

'Look, Mummy, it's a runaway digger,' she said. 'And it's eating up everything in its path. Ruuuuunn!'

'Don't panic.' Cerys swooped in and grabbed the bread, aiming it at Phoebe's mouth. 'Super Digger-girl to the rescue!' she declared, posting it deftly between Phoebe's teeth. Phoebe crowed triumphantly and punched the air. 'Come on Digger-girl,' Cerys said fondly, removing the plate from the table before a second drama could be acted out. 'Or we'll be late for school.'

'Can I say goodbye to Rico and Emma?'

'Yes, but be quick. They're busy this morning. I'll wait for you in the hall.'

'OK.' She scuttled into the shop and Cerys left the room to collect their coats from the elderly hatstand by the back door. It relied heavily on the wall for support and had now begun to list to one side. Much as she loved the old thing, Cerys had to admit that it was probably not long for this world. Propping the hatstand gently back in place, she risked a quick glance in the brass-framed mirror that hung beside it. Her hair was all over the place as usual, but no one would be able to tell the difference. Cerys teased her fingers through the worst of the tangles, aware of Phoebe's excited voice in the background, chirping happily about her part in the play. Heaven help them all if she ever decided to make a career of it, she thought, coaxing a tired smile from her reflection. I'm old, she thought suddenly, noticing deep creases about her eyes and mouth. When did that happen? I'm too young to be old. She pressed the heels of her hands into her eyes and tried to focus on her breathing. Her mother had recently joined a yoga class and claimed that proper yogic breathing had a restorative effect on the mind and body. Question was, which to try for first? Cerys was still debating when Phoebe tugged at her skirt.

'Mummy, there's no time for hide and seek. You said we'd be late.' Cerys let her hands fall and looked down into her daughter's impossibly fresh face, bursting with life. 'I'll play with you later, though,' she added, kindly. Cerys felt laughter building inside her but she pushed it down, afraid of the tears surging behind it. Once she started, she might not be able to stop, and that way lay danger.

Instead she said, 'Thanks, darling,' and ushered her child through the door she had painted happy blue, the concept suddenly contradictory in her head. Happy. Blue. Happy. Blue. Phoebe's patent leather shoes beat out the rhythm of the words as she skipped along the pavement, weaving to and fro to avoid the cracks. Happy. Blue. Cerys trailed in her wake, laden down like the little donkey of the nativity with Phoebe's various school bags and her own cares. Happy-Blue.

Was it possible to be both? Cerys squared her shoulders and bundled the thought off to the train siding in her mind, where it crowded in with the other unwelcome thoughts threatening to invade her peace.

Beth was running late for a meeting. Since it wasn't a work meeting it shouldn't have mattered. However, because it was a Nightingale meeting with Janet, it did. Janet took a dim view of lateness in all its forms, an ingrained opinion from her years as a headmistress. Sometimes Beth imagined that she was living out her retirement as she'd lived her professional years, moving on obediently as the remembered echo of an hourly bell sounded in her head. It would certainly explain why she never sat still for long, though Janet claimed it was the onset of arthritis in her knees. They were meeting at the YWCA, an imposing building on Portland Place, Oxford Circus, where Beth was a member. She had discovered it by chance and found the central location and quiet, spacious facilities ideal for the times when she needed a place to work for a few hours when she was in London. For meetings they generally hired out a room there, but today it was just the two of them, so they were meeting in the members' lounge, which was reliably quiet at this time of day. As she jogged down the busy street, dodging the slower pedestrians, her phone began to vibrate. Beth fumbled in her satchel. 'Hello?' she said breathlessly, trying to keep the same pace.

'Beth, it's Nathan. Er, are you alright? You're wheezing.'

'Fine,' she puffed. 'Bit late, that's all. You?'

'I'm good, thanks. Listen, Jen and I were wondering if you fancied coming to see Abigail in her nativity play this evening.'

'Oh, really?' Beth's heart sank.

'I mean, it won't be *Jesus Christ Superstar*, obviously, but Abigail's playing Mary and there'll be mince pies,' he said. Beth wanted to sigh but lacked the breath.

'Has Rich been onto you again?' she asked.

'What? Oh no, not at all. We just thought you might, you know, fancy getting out for the evening.'

'You're a terrible liar, Nathan.'

'I know,' he groaned. 'OK, he did give us a call. He's just worried about you being on your own, you know. But we really would love you to come.'

'Thanks, but prior . . . engagement,' gasped Beth, feeling the beginnings of a stitch in her side. She was almost there.

'Rival school nativity?'

'Handel's *Messiah* at the Albert Hall.'

'Oh, that corporate Christmas do?'

'Yeah, Rich got the tickets ages ago, sorry.' She didn't mention the heated telephone conversation in which he had practically forced her to go, saying it was pointless to waste the ticket money. 'My mum's coming instead of Rich.'

'Well, have a great time and we'll catch up soon.'

'OK, bye. Love to Jen.' She shoved the phone into her pocket as the YWCA building came into view up ahead. Beth ran into the foyer, signed herself in and clattered up the stairs, feeling clumsy and loud, as though she were running in a church or yelling in a public library. The building had the same kind of serene, dignified atmosphere that prompted you to talk in whispers. Janet was already waiting in the members' lounge, her small frame dwarfed in one of the eight high-backed sofas set in companionable twos, each pair sharing a low coffee table. It was a pleasant room, high-ceilinged and with a simplicity of arrangement that generated a sense of orderly calm. Left of the door a high, white-painted fireplace was set into the wall, its mantelpiece supported by carved wooden scrolls and flowers. Straight ahead, a series of high rectangular windows let in light and sounds of life from the street below, and a grand piano filled the space at the far corner of the room, sheaves of music placed hopefully on its stand in open invitation. A bookshelf set into the wall completed the ensemble, offering a selection of classics and contemporary fiction. Janet looked up as Beth approached.

'I always feel I've walked into the drawing-room of a Jane Austen novel when we meet here,' she said by way of greeting. 'Apart from that, of course.' She jerked her head at the small table behind the sofa, crammed with tea and coffee-making apparatus. 'Want one?'

'Coffee, please. One sugar,' Beth said gratefully, sinking into the opposite sofa. 'Sorry I'm late.'

'Not to worry,' said Janet, briskly. 'I knew you would be, so I deliberately came a quarter of an hour late myself.' She gave a tiny shudder, her steel-grey perm rippling ever so slightly as she moved her head. 'Dreadful feeling. I don't know how you cope.'

'Um. You get used to it,' Beth said, pulling a plastic file out of her satchel and tipping her working documents onto the table. 'Here, see what you think of these.' Beth's project proposal had been accepted and now, several months on, it was almost ready for implementation. The idea had grown almost organically from Beth's established trips to Uganda to help create Nightingale's annual publicity material. It was a simple idea, but one which reached beyond the children at Nightingale schools to their families and communities. During Beth's last visit, she had noticed that the children were fascinated by her photography equipment and more so by seeing their faces duplicated on a piece of paper. The majority of children had never seen a photo of themselves, and Beth had realized that this was also true of their parents and families. Good times, happy moments were recorded in memory only. Her idea was to create simple photobooks of families, including as many generations as possible. Copies could be given to each family or community group for them to keep and look back on over time, creating a shared visual memory. With permission, the best collections could also be used in fundraising material as a kind of prism through which to tell the wider story of the Nightingale community.

Together, Jane and Beth pored over the documents, discussing timeline, practicalities and funding for the project. When Beth glanced at her watch she was astonished to find that two hours had passed. 'Janet, it's 11:30,' she exclaimed. 'Didn't you say you had another appointment this morning?'

Janet leapt up as though she'd sat on a nest of wasps. 'Oh! Yes!' she said, jamming pens and paper into her bag at random. 'The dentist, 12 o'clock. I'll never make it.' Her face puckered and Beth was surprised to see she was close to tears.

'Don't worry,' she said, helping Janet on with her coat. 'Phone ahead and warn them that you're running late.'

Janet's face cleared. 'What an excellent idea,' she said, clasping Beth's hand between both of hers. 'Do you know, that would never have occurred to me. How ridiculous.'

'That's because you're never really late.'

'True,' agreed Janet. She gave a mischievous grin. 'But, you know, perhaps I'll start. It's surprisingly exhilarating. You've cured me of punctuality.' With that she took off, barrelling through the door at a run. 'I'll see you!'

'Take care, Janet,' Beth called after her, laughing as her friend vanished from sight, her red scarf trailing behind her like a woollen slipstream. The drawing-room now deserted except for her, Beth settled down to make the final adjustments to her project. By mid-afternoon she had finished, spent a guilty hour browsing on Oxford Street and was on the train back to Bookham. She pulled her phone out to send a message to her mum and realized it had been switched off since her morning meeting. 'Damn.' There were several unread texts and at least ten missed calls, most of them from her mother. Beth skipped those, knowing that each one would be at least four minutes long, garbled and identical to the one before. As well as these, there were two missed calls from Cerys. Beth frowned. It was unusual for her to call at this time of day. Without bothering to listen to the messages, she scrolled through her address book until she found her sister and hit the call button.

'Beth?'

'Yes, it's me. What's up?'

Cerys's voice sounded thick, as though she were swallowing tears. There was a pause.

'I'm . . . it's just . . . could you have a word with Phoebe?' she asked, keeping her voice low.

'Sure, is she OK?' Beth tightened her grip on the phone, becoming more concerned with every word.

'Oh, yes,' Cerys said hurriedly, obviously trying to pretend that everything was actually fine. 'It's just that it was her nativity play this afternoon and she had a big part, the angel Gabriel if you remember, and, well –' there was a brief silence as she tried to find a way of presenting the situation in its best light. 'The thing is, Martin didn't make it. Phoebe was . . . rather upset.'

'Put her on.' Beth ground her teeth, inwardly cursing her brother-in-law for his crazy work ethic, and her sister for being so disorganized. If Cerys had given her the date, she could easily have made the trip down. There was a snuffling sound as Cerys passed the phone over, then Phoebe spoke, her voice muted and sad.

'Aunty Beth?'

'Yes!' Beth boomed, causing the lady dozing beside her to jump in fright. 'Do not be afraid!'

Phoebe giggled. 'You're silly. How did you know my lines?'

'Because I was the angel Gabriel in my school nativity once, a long, long time ago,' Beth answered, determined to cheer her niece up. 'How did it go? Mummy says you were *brilliant.*'

'It was pretty good,' Phoebe said, modestly. 'Except, I was a bit too good at scaring the shepherds and Thomas Fraser had a little accident, but Miss Bloom said it was alright.'

Beth laughed. 'Start right at the beginning and tell me all about it,' she said, repositioning her legs in the cramped space and ignoring the disgruntled flick of her neighbour's newspaper as she turned the page. 'And don't forget to sing the songs. I hope you know "Little Donkey", that's my favourite.'

The private performance lasted for the rest of the train journey, continued throughout the short taxi ride from Bookham station to the cottage in Little Bookham, and finally drew to a close after two cups of tea and a slice of lemon drizzle cake while Beth huddled cross-legged by the fire with her coat on, waiting for the central heating to kick in. 'Bravo,' she said when Phoebe eventually ran out of steam. 'Well done you. Now put Mummy back on for a second.'

'OK. Love you.'

'Love you, too.' Beth wiped tears of mirth from her eyes with the corner of one mitten. An hour with Phoebe was better than a night at a comedy club.

'Hello?' Cerys came on the line, sounding brighter than before.

'Hey.'

'Thanks for that, Phoebe's perked right up.'

'So have I,' Beth said. 'She's hilarious. I wish I'd been there.'

'I know, sorry,' said Cerys. 'Been a bit . . . distracted lately. I videoed it on my phone, though.'

'Send it to Rich, he'll love it.'

'OK.' Beth waited but Cerys fell silent, the stillness on the line heavy, as if loaded with a secret meaning if only Beth could fathom it out.

'Are you sure everything's alright?' she asked tentatively.

'No. I hope so. Call me later,' Cerys said wearily, and hung up. Beth lowered the phone slowly to her lap. That didn't sound good at all. As she sat there wondering what on earth could reduce her optimistic sister to such a low ebb, the screen on the phone lit up like the Christmas star and she lifted it up, squinting at the words. Her mother always texted in capital letters and signed off as Beryl instead of Mum, as if Beth would mistake her messages for texts from someone else's mother: TERRIBLE HEAD COLD COMING ON. HAD BETTER CANCEL TONIGHT. YOU GO AND HAVE A WONDERFUL TIME!!! BERYL XX

Beth swore quietly and tossed the phone aside in disgust. 'An evening with the Stepford Wives,' she muttered, considering cancelling herself. But it was a waste of money, not to mention appearing rude, plus Rich would be cross with her. There was no escape. Beth stomped upstairs to run a bath, pretending that her only concern was the prospect of an evening of tedious company, and not the presence of David at her side. Definitely not that, she assured herself. Because why would that matter? 'No reason at all, Beth,' she said, hoping to convince herself. 'No reason at all.'

Chapter Eleven

For the third time that day, Beth was sitting on a commuter train, shuttling between Bookham and Waterloo. She sat hunched in her seat, staring out of the window from sheer habit, though it was pitch black outside and all she could see was her own reflection glowering back at her in the harsh light of the carriage. She felt the commuter's curse sweeping over her, that unpleasant *Groundhog Day* sensation, a cruel parody of déjà vu arising from an experience repeated not just once but a thousand, thousand times. Beth toyed with the idea of picking on another passenger at random and posing the question, 'Have you been here before?' simply to see the awful truth dawning on their face as they replied.

'Well, yes . . . yesterday. And the day before that and, come to think of it, twice a day every day for the last twenty years . . .'

This was precisely why city commuters adopted that lights-on-but-nobody-home blanked-out expression; not just to avoid the stress of making eye contact with strangers muscling freely into their personal space, but to avoid any conscious thought on the whole subject of commuting, lest they realize they were little more than suited hamsters in cleverly disguised wheels, and were driven mad by the revelation. Beth surveyed the carriage and grudgingly conceded that it wasn't so bad at this time of day. Most of the passengers here would be heading into London to socialize, and their faces were temporarily scrubbed clean of the greyish pallor of the hardened commuter – a combination of pollution and jaded resignation.

Not for the first time, she shuddered at the thought of a routine 9 to 5 desk job. Years ago, she had done a brief stint as an office temp and had rapidly found her brain so deadened that she felt like an automaton. Several weeks into the job she had arrived at the train station one day, smartly dressed and armed with the regulation takeaway cappuccino, only to discover after buying her ticket that it was a Saturday. She had handed in her notice the following Monday, citing self-preservation as her reason when questioned by her boss.

The carriage juddered as the train slowed for a bend in the track and Beth's head banged against the window, doing little to improve her mood. She rubbed at her forehead, tutting as her hand came away smeared with foundation. Too bad, she thought grimly, huddling deeper into her camel-coloured faux fur jacket. She had already made an enormous concession by squeezing into a black satin cocktail dress and heels she could only just walk in. Well, so far and no further. They could all just take her as she was, smudged make-up and all. It wouldn't do to look as though she'd tried too hard.

David was standing at the bar ordering a round of pre-performance drinks. He had kept an eye on the door for the last half hour, but so far there'd been no sign of Beth or her mother. As an act of faith, he decided to buy them each a gin and tonic. If the worst happened and they didn't turn up, there were plenty of other people on hand to ensure the drinks didn't go to waste. He handed his credit card to the harassed barman and turned at a gentle tug on his elbow. Harriet Fotheringham stood there, looking like an over-stuffed Christmas cracker in a red and green evening gown that bulged in all the wrong places. 'Ah, Harriet. Thank you.' Thinking she had come to help him carry some drinks, he proffered the gin and tonics.

'No, thanks,' she said, drawing back and tapping her glass of white wine with an unbelievably long fingernail. Were they false, David wondered, or were they actual talons? 'I don't drink gin.'

'Oh, OK.' Awkwardly, he splayed his fingers around the two gin glasses and his own red wine, hoping not to spill anything on his dress shirt as he jostled his way out of the drinks queue, Harriet trailing in his wake. 'So, how are you, Harriet?' he asked, attempting a jovial tone.

'Fine,' she said dismissively, her eyes scanning their group in search of her husband. 'Bill sent me to tell you that Bambi has arrived.'

'Pardon?'

'Sorry,' she said, stretching her lips into a snarl or a smile, it was unclear which. 'Just my little joke. Richard's wife is here. She's a little, ah, unsteady on her feet.'

'Do you mean she's drunk?'

Harriet gave a sharp laugh that was a cross between a bray and a bark.

'At 7:30 in the evening? I wouldn't put it past her,' she said in a confidential tone. 'But no, I was referring to her choice of footwear. Rather ill-advised, if you ask me.'

'Right, thanks, Harriet. I'll go and say hello to them.'

'There's no *them*,' Harriet said as they reached their party. 'It's just her.'

David's heart leapt into his throat and Harriet arched her eyebrows knowingly. 'So sweet of her to represent her husband, and all on her own at Christmas. Such a shame. Still, we've all been there. Hello, Beatrice!' She plunged into the group, the hem of her repulsive dress making a shimmering trail on the carpet behind her, like the tracks left by a slug. They were a large group that night, at least twenty-five from the business network plus partners or guests, and at first David couldn't spot Beth anywhere. He circled the edge of the group, exchanging distracted pleasantries and doing his best not to drop the drinks. His hands were suddenly unaccountably sweaty, and the glasses were starting to slip. He had almost completed a full circuit of the group when he found her, loitering unhappily beside a corpulent man that David didn't recognize, his scarlet cummerbund valiantly doing battle with its owner's vast paunch as he chatted to a select group of guests. David felt a surge of protectiveness as he saw that Beth wasn't included in the conversation. She looked stunning in a sleek black dress cut just above the knee, her arms folded defensively into her fake fur jacket. No wonder Harriet had been so unkind about her. With her high heels on, her legs did look as though they went on forever, even if she was swaying as she shifted her weight from foot to foot. Unconsciously David sucked in his stomach and closed the distance between them in three strides, greeting her with a kiss on the cheek and his best smile. 'Beth, hi. So good of you to come.'

'Hi, David.'

'Where's your mother?' he asked.

'I'm afraid she's feeling unwell,' Beth said.

'Oh dear, I'm so sorry,' he said, though plainly delighted. He held the trio of glasses out towards her, praying she'd be able to extract one without him dropping the lot. 'I took the liberty of getting you each a drink, but –'

'Don't worry, I'll take both.'

'Are we really that bad?' he grinned, half-appalled, half-impressed as she took a glass in each hand and drained the first in three gulps. Beth shrugged.

'I promised Rich I'd come,' she replied, diplomatically.

'How's he doing?' David asked, overenthusiastically. 'I haven't spoken to him this week.'

Another eloquent shrug. 'Oh, you know. Getting the job done.'

Instantly, he wished he hadn't mentioned it, though how could he not? The mere mention of Rich's name was enough to set an invisible wall around Beth, her expression closing to mask her loneliness.

'It looks like time to find our seats,' he said, seeing a general movement towards the door rippling through the crowded bar like a wave.

'OK, hold on.' Beth downed the second gin and tonic, ditched both glasses and shrugged out of her fur jacket. 'Ready.'

David gaped at her.

'What?' she demanded.

'Nothing, nothing,' he said, though privately stunned by this display of drinking prowess. He offered his arm and she took it, her hand resting on the sleeve of his jacket. David felt

the light pressure of her fingers so keenly it was like a brand
on his skin as they threaded their way through the crowds,
following the rest of their party. 'Er, those were double gins,
by the way,' he murmured, unable to think of anything better to say.

'I need it with all the Stepford Wives out in force.'

'Sorry?'

'Never mind.'

Beth wasn't a fan of classical choral music and so she was surprised to discover, quarter of an hour into the performance,
that she was enjoying herself. During the interval David kept
an attentive eye on her, steering her towards conversational
groups that he hoped might be of interest to her, people
with 'arty' wives or an interest in charity work. By the time
they took their seats for the second half, Beth was actively
looking forward to it. She settled back in her seat as the choir
stood and the orchestra began to play, and closed her eyes,
letting the music seep into her, permeating right through to
the fortified place where she locked up her loneliness and all
her love for Rich.

Over two months he'd been gone now, and it didn't look
like he'd be home for Christmas or New Year either. *Don't
think about it.* She fought it but the music was breaking in,
passing through the keyhole and under the door like smoke,
releasing everything inside. At Beth's right hand, David had
long since given up on the performance and simply sat
watching her, aware of every tiny detail from the smudged
make-up on her forehead to the tiny creases at the corners
of her eyes and the delicate movement of her throat as she

swallowed. If he moved his leg no more than an inch it would be touching hers. Her hands were in her lap, fingers loosely interlocked as though she were praying. As he watched her, a miracle happened. A single tear appeared and ploughed a lonely furrow down her cheek. It fell into her lap. David leaned in. 'Beth?' he said, softly. Her hand moved blindly and, finding his, clutched it tightly. 'Beth, what is it?' Her lower lip was trembling now.

'Sorry,' she whispered. David fumbled in his pocket for a handkerchief, accidentally elbowing the man on his right. Beth squeezed his hand urgently, the tears flowing freely now. 'I need to get out,' she mumbled. 'Please get me out.' David glanced to his right and saw that they were only four seats from the aisle. Thank God. Keeping tight hold of Beth's hand, he half-rose and edged past the members of the audience with repeated apologies, 'Excuse me, the lady is unwell. Excuse me, excuse me,' Beth stumbling behind him. An attendant was instantly at their side. 'Sir?'

'This lady is unwell.'

'Follow me, sir.'

David put his arm around Beth's shoulders to support her, and in a matter of moments they were out of the auditorium and into the corridor. Beth leaned against the wall, covering her eyes with her hand.

'Thank you,' David said to the attendant in polite dismissal. 'She'll be fine now.'

'Some water, sir?'

'Thank you, no.' He waited until the attendant had trotted off, her heels clipping smartly on the floor. 'Beth?' Gently he prised her hand from her eyes so that he was holding both her hands in his own, tightening his fingers on hers when she tried to pull away.

'I'm sorry,' she said again, her face a mess of streaked mascara. 'Can't seem to stop crying.' David looked at her and thought she was the most beautiful creature he had ever seen. Something twisted in him at the sight of her in such distress, and with one swift movement he pulled her into his arms. For a fraction of a second she resisted, then sagged against his chest, sobbing with renewed vigour. 'Just . . . so lonely,' she hiccupped. 'All the time lonely.'

'And being surrounded by friends is the loneliest place of all?' Beth raised her head and stared up at him, her eyes wide.

'Yes,' she murmured. 'That's it exactly. How did you . . . ?'

Quickly, before his nerve failed him, David stooped and kissed her on the brow. 'You're not alone now, Beth,' he said. 'You don't ever have to be alone.' He traced the outline of her jaw with one hand, pushing her hair gently off her face. 'Not while I'm here.'

Beth shut her eyes. Lonely . . . so lonely. And he was attractive. Overcome with emotion and fatigue, she folded into his arms. As they closed tightly around her, she knew the combination of loneliness, his persistence and the power of attraction was too much for her. It was easier to give up, give way and accept the inevitable. So she let David lead her outside and, when he turned and covered her mouth with a kiss that grew more and more demanding, she didn't resist. Lost in the intoxicating surge of want and need, any remaining guilty thoughts were finally pushed aside. At last, he drew away from her; neither of them spoke as the rain splashed down upon them. Then David hailed a cab and gave the driver his home address.

Later, Beth would look back and wonder at how shock-ingly easy it had been to begin the affair, and how quickly it gathered a momentum of its own. It was as if she had been walking a tightrope and the second her concentration lapsed she went plummeting through the air, unable to stop herself and powerless to go back. Had she known on that cold, wet December night that this was the nature of affairs she might have chosen differently. If she had realized that affairs could be ended but the weight of betrayal endured, she could have summoned the strength to draw back from the edge. If she had known how quickly events would spiral out of her con-trol . . . but she did not know, and failed to hear the sound of three lives shattering beneath her feet as she walked blindly in, abandoning her conscience in the rain.

Sixty miles away, Martin stood at the entrance to his home, a golfing umbrella sheltering him from the worst of the rain. He stood there for some time with one hand on the door-knob, the carefully composed speech creating a bitter tang in his mouth. After perhaps quarter of an hour, he pushed the door open and crossed the threshold, as though symbolically re-entering his old life for one last time. He left the um-brella dripping on the hatstand, removed his coat and shoes and climbed the stairs on silent feet. It was late and he was unsure whether or not Cerys would still be awake, but when he entered their bedroom she was standing by the window with her back to him. The room was dark except for the small clip-on reading light she kept fixed to the headboard of the bed, the light illuminating the outline of her shoulder blades jutting through the thin fabric of her dressinggown. Martin crossed the room and kissed the top of her head, on the spot where the whorls of her double crown spiralled away from one another. Cerys froze. 'So.'

'So.'

'I tried all morning to reach you,' she said, quietly. 'And all afternoon.'

'I'm sorry.'

'Phoebe was excellent, by the way. You would have been so proud.'

'I *am* proud.' A car swished by on the road below, splashing gutter water onto the pavement.

'Where were you?'

'In a meeting.'

'Were you really in a meeting?' There was no accusation in her voice, only a tedious desire to hear the truth. Out of the corner of his eye, Martin glimpsed a suitcase placed in readiness by the wardrobe and saw that his news was not news after all. The confession had already been written and all that was required of him was a signature at the bottom.

'No,' he said. She crossed her arms tightly across her stomach as if to prevent her guts from spilling out onto the cream carpet. Unable to see her face, Martin waited.

'How long?'

'Not long. A few . . . a few months,' he said, wanting to be truthful while knowing that nothing he said would be believed, now or ever again. After feeding her lies, she was hardly going to swallow the truth. They stood in silence, Martin nervously trying to gauge his wife's reaction from the set of her shoulders. Cerys lifted the net curtain and gazed out into the dark for a long time, watching the wind spit fat raindrops onto the glass. Cloud tears, Phoebe called them. Eventually she let the curtain fall.

'Go,' was all she said. Martin hesitated, torn between the desire to make a quick getaway and the perverse need to explain, to articulate his guilt, perhaps offload some of it onto her. Before he could speak, Cerys flicked one hand out, indicating the suitcase.

'Go,' she repeated. Martin picked up the case and left the room, glancing back in the doorway, certain she would at least turn to watch him leave. Cerys gave him nothing. She remained like a statue as he walked out of her world, staring fixedly out into the dark long after he had gone.

When her limbs had grown stiff and her fingers ached with the cold, Cerys roused herself sufficiently to shuffle over to the bed. She climbed in with slow, halting movements and lay down, drawing the covers over herself like a shroud as the life she had known died and everything turned to dust.

Chapter Twelve

Beth stood in the bathroom, carefully examining her face in the mirror for signs of deceit. Oddly, there were none. Perhaps it took longer than a month and a half for them to show. Her skin glowed, her eyes were clear and bright and she looked a picture of health. In fact, people were telling her she'd never looked so well. *How could lying be good for you?* she wondered, pulling David's bathrobe more securely around her. In the bedroom her phone rang, and David poked his head round the door. 'Catch,' he grinned, sending it across the room with an underarm lob. Beth dived for it and just managed to catch it before it fell into the bath.

'Hello?' she said, perching on the porcelain rim and mouthing, 'Go away,' at David. He loitered, waiting to see who the call was from. 'Oh, hi, Mum,' Beth said brightly, flapping her free hand at him. 'Yes, fine, thanks. How are you?' Satisfied that it wasn't Rich, David slouched back into the bedroom. Beth got up and pushed the door to with her foot to mask the sound of him whistling as he got dressed. 'You want to drive down to Brighton today?' Her heart sank. David had planned a day out and wasn't going to be pleased if she cancelled at a moment's notice. Despite the clandestine nature of their time together, or perhaps because of it, he was becoming increasingly jealous of any free time of Beth's that wasn't devoted to him. She found it hard to handle. Rich was never like that.

'Elizabeth?'

'Yes, I'm here.'

'What do you think?'

'Er . . .' She pushed her hair off her face and tried to concentrate on the conversation. 'Sorry, run that past me again, Mum.'

'I was *saying*,' her mother said, crossly, 'if we drove down in the afternoon we could spend a few hours with Phoebe while Cerys is working, then I thought perhaps you might take your sister out for dinner?' She hesitated for a second, then pressed on. 'I could babysit.' Beth's eyes widened at this pronouncement. Their mother hated babysitting, even for Phoebe, because she claimed it made her feel like Cinderella, home alone while others were out having fun. She must be very worried about Cerys to make the offer.

'Are you sure, Mum?'

'Perfectly. I thought I'd bring a friend, you know, and we can play cards once Phoebe's gone to bed.'

'Who?' Beth asked, thinking *not Beatty, please God, not Beatty. Let it be Emily or Christine, even Margot, just not Beatty.*

'Beatty. I did ask Christine, but she's playing Bridge tonight.'

'Excellent,' Beth groaned.

'Are you alright, dear? You sound as though you're in pain.'

'Just a bit of indigestion,' Beth answered, closing her eyes as the entire weekend collapsed about her like a house of cards. 'So I'll pick you up at, what, 3 o'clock?'

'If you would, darling. I'll make sure Beatty's here in good time.'

'Great. But listen, Mum,' Beth said, trying to inject an authoritative note into her voice. 'I'm not taking Cerys out to pump her for information, right? She'll talk when she's ready.'

'Of course not, darling,' her mother replied, sounding hurt. 'Just see if you can get her to open up a bit, that's all. Tell you what happened and so forth. She and Martin were together for years.'

'Mum . . .' Beth said warningly.

'Oops, toast's burning! See you at three.'

Beth plodded back into the bedroom, where David was lying on the bed with his hands tucked behind his head in an effort to appear nonchalant.

'Day out's off then,' he said, not bothering to pretend he hadn't been listening in.

Beth sat down on the edge of the bed. 'I'm afraid so.' She tried to stroke his cheek but he flinched away. 'Don't be like that,' she pleaded. 'It's not my fault.'

He rolled away from her. 'You could have said no.'

'With what excuse?' she demanded, feeling her temper ignite. 'Sorry, Mum, but I'm having an affair and that's more important than my sister, who, incidentally, seems on the edge of a nervous breakdown?'

'Sure, rub it in, why don't you?' he retorted. 'I know I'm bottom of the list.'

'That is not true!' Beth spluttered. 'But this is *family*, David.' She crossed to the dressing table and snatched up her brush, yanking it through her hair. 'What do you expect?' He rolled off the bed and came to stand behind her, their eyes meeting in the mirror.

'I don't *expect* anything, Beth,' he spat. 'What I hope – hoped, I should say – was that you loved me the way I love you. That you wanted to make time for me, us.'

'David . . .'

'Forget it.' He spun away from her and stalked to the door. 'I'm going out. Call me when you have a window in your diary. If you can fit me in at all, that is.'

Beth stood rooted to the spot as he slammed the door. Before she could gather her wits the front door was slamming too, and David was gunning the engine in his car. She ran to the window in time to see him clear the corner with a reckless skid. Then he was gone and she was alone in his bedroom, the silence ringing with echoes of his anger. Beth clutched at her chest, the injustice of his words robbing her of breath. The room was tidy, ordered and calm like its owner, from the sleek double bed, so low that it was almost a futon, to the floating shelves and the glass-topped dressing table with its round sunburst mirror hovering on the wall above. The only signs of disarray came from Beth's things. Last night's clothes like a stain on the grey carpet, cosmetics scattered across the dressing table, her silk chemise lolling insolently on the end of the bed as if to say, 'Fold up neatly? Make me.'

'Right,' Beth said, breathing deeply to calm her anger. 'Right. Stuff you.' If David wanted everything in his life to be tidy and controlled, he could have it. She burst into action, pulling a floral holdall from the bottom of the wardrobe and moving about the room, clearing her belongings from every inch of the place with dramatic sweeps of her arm. She pulled open the drawer where she knew David had hidden a photo of Carlotta and slapped it back in place on his ridiculous cube-shaped bedside cabinet that was no more than a framed hole with a few books stacked inside. It was the sort of furniture that impressed her mother. 'Well, not me,' she raged. 'Not any more.'

She clattered down the stairs, stole her coat, hat and scarf from the pegs in the hallway and stormed out. Her departure was a carbon copy of David's, right down to the skid at the end of the road, though this turned out to be a patch of ice rather than an emotional statement. On a positive note, it served to shock Beth out of her temper and averted a dangerous, rage-fuelled drive from South Kensington back to Little Bookham.

Driving sensibly now, the radio shrill above the drone of the heater, Beth saw the row for what it was. She had learned to read David quickly and it was perfectly obvious what was bothering him. They were now into early February. Rich had been away for three months, shuttling between the apartment in Aktobe and the gas field in Karachaganak. His work would be finished soon, and even if it were to be extended he would be given some home leave. Globe Oil had a relatively strict policy on foreign postings in that respect. David knew this. It was clear that he wanted to make the most of the time they had left.

'Because it will all be over then,' Beth said aloud, her gloved fingers drumming nervously on the steering-wheel like leather-clad spider legs. 'Over and done.' If she said it often enough then it would happen that way. Easy to say when she was angry with David, and safely out of range of his magnetism. 'Over and done,' she repeated, unable to think of how this would come to pass, only that it must. She turned up the radio, drowning out the voice in the back of her head and its unwelcome, whispered truths. *An affair is an affair whether your husband is at home or not, Beth. What difference does his whereabouts make?* But it did, she thought, hot tears of shame welling in her eyes. It did make a difference. 'You should never have left me, Rich,' she wept, the road ahead as blurred as the future. 'Why did you go away?' *But he's been away many times before,* the voice pressed, hurting her now. *Many times and you've never strayed. It's got nothing to do with him.* Beth shook her head, denying her conscience, denying it all. *Practising, are you?*

'Shut. Up.' It was no good, she realized in a moment of clarity. Shameful as her position was, if she didn't share her predicament with someone she would drive herself mad. The trouble was, the only person she could trust 100 per cent was her sister and Cerys might not be up to it. Best to decide when she saw her in the flesh. Blocking out everything but the road ahead, Beth drove on.

David was still angry. He had driven around London for nearly an hour, pumped with fury. He was not a man used to being refused. Once he calmed down and was able to think straight he would realize he had behaved like an idiot. He knew that Cerys had left her husband just before Christmas and that Beth was deeply concerned about her sister, not least because Cerys had given her family no more than the bare facts of their separation, no reasons, nothing. In time he would apologize and beg Beth's forgiveness. At this precise moment, however, he was gripped by a need to retaliate. It was a mean, petty response which was wholly unworthy of him, but there just the same. He pulled into a side road, swung the car into the kerb and grabbed his phone from the passenger seat.

'Amanda? Hi!' he said, projecting all his charm into the greeting. 'Listen, you aren't at a loose end by any chance, are you? Only, I'm heading over to Oxford for the day, and I wondered if you'd like to join me. There's a fantastic gastro pub just opened on the outskirts. You'd love it.' He grinned broadly. 'You would? Great. Give me your postcode and I'll be right over. Yeah, can't wait.' He punched the address into his Sat Nav and drove off, already visualizing the look on Beth's face later. In fact, he might not even take her call.

Cerys slumped forward in the car so that her head was resting on the dashboard. 'That woman is . . . is . . .'

'A motormouth? Insufferable? Opinionated?' Beth suggested.

'All of those,' Cerys said, weakly. 'And she cheats at cards. I saw her hand as we were leaving.'

'Let's hope Phoebe doesn't notice,' said Beth, starting the engine and flicking her wipers on. 'Or Mum, for that matter.' It was raining again, malicious winter rain with shards of ice that stung cheeks and slid slyly beneath upturned collars to melt against unguarded skin. She shivered and put the heater on full blast. 'I hate this time of year,' she said, steering through the evening traffic. 'There's no point to winter once Christmas is over, and it still feels like ages until spring.'

'I know what you mean.'

'So how's things?'

'Yeah, ticking over.'

Beth glanced at her sister. Cerys had got very good at banal comments lately, saying just enough to keep a conversation going while avoiding anything that could be construed as meaningful.

'You don't need to worry,' she said. 'I'm not reporting back to base at the end of the evening.'

'That's good,' answered Cerys vaguely, staring out of the window. 'Rain looks nasty.' Beth waited until they reached the restaurant, a little Italian place that Cerys had recommended, and were seated at their table, studying a pair of slightly dog-eared menus. Then she tried again.

'Look,' she said earnestly, trying and failing to reach her sister's hand across the table. 'We're worried about you, Mum and me. And we're worried about Phoebe, too.'

'She never saw Martin that much anyway, with his job the way it was,' Cerys murmured, her eyes fixed on her menu. 'Phoebe's fine.'

'But you're not fine, Cerys,' Beth said, gently. 'You're not.' Cerys maintained a mutinous silence. 'Cerys, anything you tell me isn't going to go any further –'

'But may be used as evidence against me in the Court of Mum?'

'No! I promise.' Beth set her menu down and met her sister's gaze, sharp and accusing. 'Mum wants to know what the score is, of course she does, but I know what she's like as well as you do, and if you think I'd go tittle-tattling to her you're way off the mark.' Cerys fiddled with her napkin, looking unsure. Beth folded her arms on the table. 'Here's what I think,' she said, quietly. 'One, you're badly hurt, more than you want to admit, and you don't want to discuss it. That's fine. Two, something kicked off, because husbands and wives don't just separate for no reason, especially when they've got a child. You don't want to discuss that either. And three –' she leaned forward, watching her sister carefully. 'Three, the fact that you don't want to discuss it means either that you think Mum would go ape or that we'd be in some way disappointed in you. And that's *not* fine because it isn't true.' She sat back in her chair and waited.

'That's what you think, is it?' Cerys picked up a cocktail stick and helped herself to a complimentary olive from the earthenware dish in the centre of the table. 'Well, what I think is it's a good job you're a photographer and not a detective. Oh, hi,' she said as a waiter appeared at her elbow. 'One garlic bread pizza with tomato to start, please, and then two of the goat's cheese and sundried tomato pizzas to follow.' She paused for a second, frowning at the menu. 'One side salad, one portion of chips and two cokes as well, please. Thank you.'

Beth handed her menu back to the waiter with a shrug, torn between amusement and irritation. Clearly she wasn't being given any choice where dinner was concerned. Cerys went back to eating olives, staring at the red and white checked tablecloth as though it was the most fascinating thing she'd ever seen. 'Heard from Rich lately?' she asked, idly.

'Yesterday,' Beth said, batting the question away with her hand. She eyed her sister closely, debating whether or not to take the risk. If her theory was correct she would be on safe ground. 'OK, Cerys. There was something I wanted to talk to you about myself, sooo . . .' she crossed two fingers on each hand and made a third cross shape on the table, laying her left wrist diagonally over her right.

Cerys laughed. 'What, our old "Trade Secrets" pact? One from you, one from me –'

'– and parents none the wiser,' Beth finished, falling into the rhythm of the old chant that they used to seal the deal as children. 'What do you say?' Conversation stopped as the waiter arrived with their drinks and the starter. After a couple of deliberately slow mouthfuls of coke, Cerys dabbed at her mouth with a napkin and nodded. 'OK,' she said. 'But as a matter of fact, I was planning to tell you anyway.'

'You were?'

'I'm not an idiot, Beth,' Cerys said. 'And I'm sorry if you feel I've been shutting you out.'

'You are?'

'Of course I am.' She offered the plate of garlic bread to Beth, taking two slices for herself. 'I just needed some time to concentrate on Phoebe and to get my own head round everything before getting this out in the open. To be honest, I don't think it would be healthy to bottle it all up for too long. I don't want Mum to know just yet, but I reckon I'd go mad if I never spoke about it.' In point of fact, she had told someone, but Beth would be hurt to learn that Cerys had turned elsewhere for support. There was no need for her to know about the tearful Christmas Eve phone call to Jenny, made late at night from her old bedroom at their family home after everyone had gone to bed.

Beth's face relaxed. 'I know exactly where you're coming from,' she said, fervently. 'It's awful trying to hold something in.' She toyed with the dainty silver cross that she often wore around her neck and smiled at her sister, amazed at the symmetry of their lives. 'You've met someone else, haven't you?' she guessed, feeling an absurd delight at the idea that they were both simultaneously going through the same experience.

'Don't be an idiot, Beth,' Cerys said, hotly. 'Credit me with a little more integrity than that. Martin was the one having an affair.'

Beth's mouth fell open. 'M–Martin?' she stammered.

'Yes,' said Cerys, bluntly. 'Good old honest, reliable Martin.'

'I'm . . . stunned,' Beth said, feeling as if her brain had been cannoned into the air and was tumbling back into her head in jumbled fragments.

'All those long days, the late evening meetings that he told me were overtime to get more commission,' Cerys went on, bitterness twisting her mouth into an ugly, puckered shape. 'And all the time he was with *her*, whoever she is.'

'But who is she?'

'I don't know yet, and frankly I don't care. Some tart or other. Does it matter?'

'I suppose not.' Beth felt an insane urge to defend the woman, to say that she might not be all that bad, that sometimes these things just happen. Looking at the fire in her sister's eyes she bit the words back, mortified at misreading the situation so badly. Cerys mistook her discomfort for shock, and gave her a crooked smile. 'Sorry to dump that on you,' she said, mopping the last of the garlic butter off her plate. 'I know it's a bit of a shock. You can see why I'm reluctant to tell Mum. It's better that she thinks we just decided to go our separate ways for now.'

Beth nodded, keeping her head down as a guilty blush burned across her face. Beryl adored Martin. The waiter collected their plates and presented their pizzas with a flourish which both women ignored. He flounced away, gesticulating at his colleagues that tips were unlikely to come from that table.

'The hardest part,' Cerys went on conversationally, 'is that he must have been lying to me for months.' She heaved a sigh, holding herself together with admirable self-control. 'I suppose it just goes to show that you can never truly know a person, or what they're capable of.'

Beth kept her eyes on her plate, watching the slices of melted goat's cheese congealing over the oily sundried tomatoes. 'So. Your turn,' Cerys said, attacking her pizza as if it were the face of Martin's mistress. Beth panicked.

'What? Oh, I'll tell you later,' she stammered, gripping her cutlery so tightly that her fingers began to cramp. Cerys raised her knife and pointed the blade at her sister, pretending to take aim. 'No way,' she said. 'We had a deal. Fess up.' Beth blinked at her sister, horrified at the position she'd put herself in. There was no spin she could put on her version of events, no gloss that would lacquer over her tawdry actions. Worst of all, she couldn't bear the prospect of losing her sister's good opinion of her. Cerys waited, the knife still poised. 'Spill,' she commanded. Beth was in agony. *Say something. Say something. Anything.* Her mind was empty of everything but the truth.

'We're going to try for a baby,' she blurted. 'When Rich gets home, I mean.'

Cerys dropped her knife with a clatter. 'That's it?' she spluttered. 'You bigged up the whole secret thing and that's it?'

'Yeah,' Beth said, forcing a laugh. 'Pretty lame compared to your news, I know. Best I had.'

'I'll say,' Cerys agreed, signalling the waiter for more drinks. 'Congratulations and all, but I think I win.'

'No arguments there,' Beth said weakly, hiding her shaking hands in her lap.

'I can't believe I fell for the old "I've got a big secret" line.'

'I'll pay for dinner to make up for it.'

'Too right you will. You're a dirty cheat, Beth Hampton.'

Chapter Thirteen

In the dingy bedroom of his rented apartment in Aktobe, Kazakhstan, Rich woke at midnight with the bizarre sensation of his pillow vibrating. Fumbling in the dark, he extracted his mobile and put it to his ear. 'Hello?' he croaked, dimly aware of the sound of sobbing in the background.

'Where have you *been*?' a voice screeched in his ear. 'I've been calling all day –'

'Beth?'

'Calling and calling and you weren't there!' she sobbed.

'I – I'm sorry, my battery was dead,' Rich stammered, unable to get his tired brain up to speed. 'I left it charging in the apartment today.'

'But I left messages!'

'I didn't have my phone,' Rich said, patiently. 'I didn't check it when I got in, love, I'm sorry. Tell me what's wrong.'

Beth took a deep, shuddering breath. 'You have to come home.'

'What?'

'Please, Rich,' Beth gulped. 'You have to come home right now.'

'What . . . wait a minute . . .' Rich sat up and snapped on the bedside light. 'What's happened? Are you OK?'

'No, I'm not OK. Please, Rich, I'm begging you.'

'Beth, calm down. You have to tell me what the problem is.'

'It isn't – I can't –'

'Deep breaths –'

'PLEASE!' she wailed. 'I just need you to come home.' She burst into uncontrollable sobs. Rich dropped the phone onto the duvet and rubbed his eyes with both hands, blinking stupidly at the screen. What the hell was going on?

'Rich?'

He grabbed the phone. 'Look, just – hold on a second, alright? Don't go away. I'm getting up.' Rich got out of bed and stumbled into the bathroom to splash cold water on his face, his reflection tired and grainy in the mirror. Propped by the hot tap, the mobile projected Beth's weeping into the sink, sending tinny echoes of her tears down the plughole. Rich pressed a towel to his face, scooped the phone up and returned to the bedroom. 'Right,' he said, climbing back into bed. 'I'm here. Whatever's wrong, we'll sort it out, OK?'

'OK,' Beth hiccupped. 'I love you.'

'I love you too, sweetheart.' There was silence on the line as Beth's breathing began to settle into a more normal rhythm. Rich sent up a silent prayer of thanks. He didn't do hysterics at the best of times, and certainly not long distance. After a minute or so, he judged it safe to proceed. 'Better?' he asked.

'A bit.'

'OK. So tell me.'

'Rich, I just miss you so much,' she said, her voice no more than a whisper on the line. 'I can't do this any more, I'm not coping.'

Rich leaned back, the whitewashed wall cold and unyielding behind his head. 'I'm not coping brilliantly either,' he sympathized. 'But it won't be long now, just a few more weeks and I'll be home.'

'You've been saying that since the day you left.'

'I know, but I really mean it this time. We're almost there,' said Rich. 'I can't leave without finishing the job; it wouldn't be right. Just a few more weeks, I promise, Beth.'

'I can't wait a few weeks,' she said, despair dulling her voice.

'Yes, you can,' he insisted, determined to raise her spirits. 'And then I promise you I'll never leave again.' He closed his eyes as Beth began to cry once more. 'Please don't cry,' he begged. 'I already feel like the worst husband in the world.'

'You're not,' she said through her tears. 'You're the best husband, the best. Please come home.'

'Beth, you know that I can't. I took the job and I have to see it through. Please understand.'

'There must be other people who could do it,' she insisted, stubbornly. 'People who could finish it off.'

'David asked me,' Rich said, quietly. 'Not other people. Me.' This prompted a fresh bout of hysterics from the English end of the line. Rich started to panic. 'Beth, is there something else?' he asked, raising his voice to be heard above her tears. 'This isn't like you. Is it Cerys?'

'Cerys . . . David . . . all of them,' she sobbed. 'It's everything, everything. Come home.'

'Beth, listen. Listen to me,' Rich insisted as she tried to talk over him. 'I want you to make a cup of tea and go to bed. Please. You're overwrought and you sound exhausted. Call me tomorrow when you wake up. I promise I'll have my phone with me.' She didn't reply, but Rich thought the crying was a bit less shrill. 'Will you do that?' he pressed, hoping she'd say yes since he had no better solution to suggest. Beth wouldn't thank him for sending her mother round, and Cerys had enough problems of her own. Besides, he wasn't sure anyone could reason with her in this state. 'Beth?'

'I love you,' she wept. 'I love you so much, Rich.'

'I love you, too. Go to bed now, alright? OK? You'll feel better in the morning.'

'OK,' she whispered. 'Bye.' Rich shut the phone off and lay down, staring up at the ceiling, knowing there was more to this. But what could he do to comfort his beautiful wife from here? How could he make it better? Whatever 'it' was. It took a long time to get back to sleep.

At 10:30 the following morning, David pushed his computer keyboard away from him and checked his phone for messages. Again. In the three weeks since he and Beth had rowed, it had become like a nervous tic that he couldn't cure. That and leaving messages for her, not just texts but long, pleading voicemails that left him feeling unmanly and humiliated. She had ignored them all. David stared miserably at the blank screen, wishing that he could have just five minutes with her, certain that he could put things right between them. The phone on his desk trilled and he picked it up automatically. 'David Samuel.'

'Sorry to bother you, sir, but there's a lady in reception for you.'

'I've no appointments this morning,' he barked, unable to rein his temper in, though he knew he was shooting the messenger. 'I asked not to be disturbed.'

'Sir, I know,' stammered the hapless woman. 'I explained that, but she's, er, er –'

'Spit it out, damn it.'

'Rather insistent on seeing you,' she managed. 'Sir.'

'Well, that's too bad,' David replied curtly. 'Take a message and politely get rid of her.'

'I've already tried that, sir,' gulped the secretary. 'She's refusing to leave.' David threw his mobile into the desk drawer and slammed it shut.

'Then she can stay sitting there until the mountains fall and the hills turn to dust,' he shouted. 'Who is this woman?'

'Mrs Hampton, sir,' squeaked the secretary.

David's jaw dropped. 'Richard Hampton's wife? *That* Mrs Hampton?'

'Yes, sir. I'll pass your message on, sir.'

'No! Send her up immediately. Immediately, please.' David was on his feet, the phone cord stretched to its limit before he realized he was still holding the receiver. 'Have you offered her coffee? See that she has a coffee, a tea, whatever she wants. Send her up. And thank you, Rebecca.'

'It's Roberta, sir.'

'Her too.' David hung up and strode to the door of his office, then changed his mind and returned to his desk. It wouldn't do to look too keen, he told himself, then dismissed the thought as pathetic before it was fully formed, and rose to his feet just as Beth barrelled into the room, her eyes wild.

'Twenty-one voicemail messages and at least as many texts and then you refuse to see me?' she said, glaring at him.

'I can't apologize enough,' David said, hurrying to close the door, desperate to hold her again. 'I had no idea it was you.'

Beth stepped away from him as he approached, folding her arms in a defensive posture to prevent him from getting into her space. Because once he got close to her, she knew she'd never be able to resist him.

'Beth, darling –'

'I'm not here for you,' she interrupted him, taking the seat opposite his desk. 'I'm here for Rich, and I don't have much time.'

'OK.' David moved around the desk and took his seat, wary of this decisive, businesslike Beth. 'What can I do?'

'You need to recall Rich,' she said, firmly. 'Now, right away. I want you to do it today.'

David was already shaking his head before the words were out of her mouth. 'Not possible, Beth.'

'It's possible if you want it to be,' she replied. David spread his hands and smiled apologetically as if to say *Yes, but I don't want it to be.*

'I'm afraid it's out of the question,' he said, smoothly. 'But Rich will be home in a matter of weeks now. I'm sure he's told you that himself.'

'He has,' she said, shifting her purple leather handbag onto her knee and opening the clasp. 'It's not soon enough.'

'Are you saying this to hurt me?' David asked suddenly, dropping his corporate smile and gazing at her with unchecked longing. 'To punish me? How many times can I apologize to you?' Beth's heart contracted at the expression on his face but she forced herself to remain blank, professional. 'Beth,' David said, softly. 'I'm begging you. Don't you love me at all?'

'It's irrelevant, David,' she said. 'We made a mistake, a big one. It's not too late to put it right.'

'You came all this way to tell me that?'

'No,' she said, fishing in her bag. 'I came to tell you this.' She withdrew a slim white plastic stick and dropped it onto the desk. David leaned forward, frowning.

'Is that . . .'

'A pregnancy test, yes,' she said, briskly. 'With two blue lines.' David flopped back, his head striking the back of his padded leather chair. The room swam.

'You can't always tell from one,' he said, faintly. Beth reached into her bag and produced a fistful of the incriminating sticks.

'Six,' she said grimly. 'You can tell from six.'

At that moment, the door opened and the secretary trotted in with a heavily laden tray. 'Coffee?' she announced brightly, the cafetiere slipping dangerously towards the edge of the wobbling refreshment tray as she crossed the room. Beth recovered first, scooping the evidence into her handbag and moving aside to make way for the drinks. When the secretary had left, tripping and banging her tray against the doorframe as her heel caught in the carpet, David and Beth faced each other silently across the table. Beth pressed the plunger on the cafetiere and poured the coffee.

'It's not too late,' she said again, pushing one cup towards David. 'If you call Rich home now, nobody need ever know.'

'I'll know,' David said. 'You'll know.'

Beth inclined her head, acknowledging the hit. 'We'll just have to find a way to live with it,' she replied. 'Make amends somehow.'

David eyed her over the rim of his cup. How did you make amends for falling in love with your friend's wife and

fathering her child? Besides, making amends implied regret
– and David wasn't sorry. 'How?' he asked, simply.

Beth was ready with her answer. 'For you? By giving the
child up,' she declared. It was a good answer. David blinked
owlishly at her, unable to conjure a counter-argument. 'I
love Rich,' she went on, pre-empting David's next question.
'I won't leave him. Not ever.'

'And me?'

'Well, you've got Amanda, haven't you?' she answered,
tartly.

'Beth, please.'

'No, David,' she said vehemently, her hair falling across her
eyes as she shook her head. 'It's over. We'll move away, Rich
and me, get new jobs. We were planning to in any case.' Beth
bit her lip as David put his head in his hands, knowing that
everything hung in the balance. If Rich had complied and
come home, David need never have known. If Beth could
have gone through with an abortion, *no one* need ever have
known. She'd looked up a clinic but found herself unable to
physically make the call. Whoever else was to blame, it certainly wasn't the unborn child. As it was, she had been left
with no choice but to throw herself on David's mercy. Her
only hope was the old ties of friendship and whatever honour David had in him. 'It has to be over,' she repeated. 'Surely
you can see that?' David raised his head and Beth saw a
glimpse of the titanic struggle between what he wanted and
what he knew he ought to do. Eventually he spoke, forcing
the right words past lips that fought to hold them in.

'I do see it,' he mumbled. 'I don't want to, but I do.'

'So you'll call Rich home?'

David nodded, pierced by the rejection. 'The baby,' he mumbled.

'That's a sacrifice you have to make,' Beth said, swiftly. 'You've had your family, David. This would crush Rich if he knew.'

'It's crushing me.'

'And me,' she said. He saw that her hand was trembling as she set her cup down, and felt a brief surge of hope at the pain in her face. But when she spoke again, her voice was level, her words implacable, like bullets in his heart. 'But the difference is, David, we deserve it. Rich doesn't.' Her eyes filled with tears. 'I love him so much.'

'I love you,' David said, appalled at the desperation in his voice.

'And I love you,' she replied, quietly, standing and gathering her things. 'I really do, David. I love you both, in different ways. But I loved him first, and my promises were to him.'

'Beth,' he said, brokenly, 'don't leave me. Everybody leaves me. Jonathan, Carlotta . . . I can't bear it if you go too.'

'Forgive me.'

'Don't go.' But she did, leaving only her perfume lingering faintly in the air, subtle and elusive like remembered happiness.

Chapter Fourteen

1 WEEK. HE WON'T COME ANY SOONER.

Beth pressed the reply button on her phone and typed a question. The reply came in under a minute: PROBLEM WITH USA AND LOCALS OVER WELLS.

Frowning, Beth considered this. HOW HARD DID YOU TRY? she sent.

VERY.

I'LL TRY AGAIN THEN.

DON'T. CAN'T RISK LINKING HIS RECALL DIRECTLY TO YOU. 1 WEEK OK?

HAVE TO BE WON'T IT.

I'M SORRY.

Beth didn't bother to reply.

'We're all sorry,' she muttered, switching the phone off so that she could justifiably miss any calls David might make. 'But that doesn't make it OK, does it.' She trudged through to the kitchen, flicked the kettle on and sat down at the table, where her diary lay open, several dates ringed in red. Beside it was a notepad with various scribbled calculations on it. This date would mean six weeks pregnant, that one, eight. 'Of course,' the midwife had said cheerily, 'modern pregnancy tests are so sensitive that you could be as little as five or even four weeks. It all depends on the dates. I know it's a bind, but it really does pay to keep track of your periods.'

'It all depends on the dates,' Beth repeated, staring at the notepad. Even her handwriting looked panicky, she thought, seeing guilt in everything she said or did. 'And not just my dates.' She gnawed the end of the pen anxiously, trying to tally up the various possibilities. One week until Rich came home. If she was still in the earliest stages of pregnancy, say five weeks, she would get away with it, leave it as long as possible to 'discover' she was pregnant and make sure Rich didn't come to any of the ante-natal appointments. With any luck she might be overdue, and the baby small. Cerys had been two weeks over before finally going into labour, Beth remembered. That would help. Suddenly she threw the pen down and covered her face with her hands. It was hopeless. All these ifs and buts and nothing firm to take hold of. She'd have more luck catching rain in a sieve.

Bracing both hands on the table, she hauled herself upright as though she were already eight months pregnant, and shuffled over to the kettle. So tired, she thought, her brain hardly able to form a coherent thought. Intent on siphoning resources into the rapidly developing foetus, her body was sparing enough energy to keep itself ticking over, no more. 'I could sleep for a hundred years,' Beth yawned. A loud knock at the back door put paid to that idea.

'Ow!' Scalding water slopped over the rim of her mug and splashed on her hand. 'Just a minute!' she yelled, wrapping a damp dishcloth round her fingers. She opened the door and found Jenny and Nathan on the doorstep in matching exercise gear, their faces flushed and glowing from exertion.

'Surprise!' said Jenny.

'Uh, yeah,' said Beth. 'Come in.' She moved back to allow them in. 'Just making a cuppa,' she said, waving her wrapped hand. 'I'll put the kettle on, shall I?' Her lack of enthusiasm was more obvious than she intended. Jenny hesitated on the threshold.

'Are you sure?' she asked. 'I know we've called by unannounced, but we were out anyway and . . .'

'What she means,' Nathan interrupted, his head poking over Jenny's shoulder as he stood on the doorstep behind her, 'is that we got a sitter so we could play badminton, and having escaped, we want to make the most of it.' He gave Beth a conspiratorial wink. 'Also, we'd booked the court for an hour and a half, and Jenny was done in after twenty minutes.'

'I was not!'

'And she was losing.'

Beth beckoned them both in, smiling properly for the first time in weeks. She knew they were here to check up on her but tired as she was, she found herself glad of their easy company.

'Ah well,' she said. 'To the victor the spoils, but the loser gets the biggest slice of cake.'

'What an excellent rule,' Jenny said, plonking herself down at the table. 'We should introduce that at home, Nathan.'

'Are you kidding? Abigail would tear us limb from limb.' Nathan shrugged his jacket off and shooed Beth away from the kettle. 'I'll do that,' he said. 'You look done in.'

'I am, actually,' Beth admitted, fetching the cake tins before collapsing beside Jenny. 'You don't mind if I pass on plates, do you?'

'Not at all,' Jenny said, prising the lid off the tin and greedily eyeing the selection of muffins. 'I won't be leaving any crumbs.' She smiled up at Nathan as he ferried the mugs of tea over to the table. 'Isn't this bliss? A few hours off duty and a visit thrown in.'

'Sure is,' Nathan agreed. 'Tea and cake with lashings of comfort and joy.'

'Lashings of comfort and joy,' Beth echoed. 'What a peculiar saying. I've never heard that before.'

'It's a Jonathan-ism,' Jenny said. 'An old friend of ours from university.'

'He loved his food, Jonathan did,' sighed Nathan, devouring a chocolate muffin in two huge bites. Beth pushed the tin towards him, David's words coming back to her with a jolt. 'Everybody leaves me.' Almost the last thing he said to her as he begged her not to go.

'Tell me about Jonathan,' she said, suddenly.

Alone in his too-large sitting-room, David was eating a microwave meal. It was supposed to be spaghetti Bolognese, but as he twirled the stodgy strands of pasta around on his plate in an effort to wind them onto his fork, David wished he hadn't bothered. It looked nothing like any Bolognese he'd ever tasted, and the cardboard packaging probably contained more nutritional value than its dubious contents. 'Come on,' he told himself encouragingly. 'You've got to eat something.' He carried his plate to the kitchen and held it over the bin, watching the awful stuff slither over the rim, inch by inch. 'Yuck.' An involuntary shudder ran through him. A brief inspection of his food supplies revealed copious amounts of cheese, a few tins of soup, some oat crackers and rather a lot of Shredded Wheat. Why on earth had he bought so much of that? And when? 'Cheese and biscuits,' he decided, fetching himself a large glass of red wine to accompany it.

David tried to settle down again in front of the television, but gave up after several minutes of fruitless channel-hopping, and got up. Full of nervous energy, he roamed aimlessly about the house, his plate balanced on the palm of one hand, sitting on the stairs for a while, then going upstairs to his study and back down to the kitchen again to top up his wine glass. Eventually he tired of this as well, and decided he should have a bath to unwind. When the bath was half full he changed his mind, emptied it all and went into his bedroom, closing the door firmly behind him. 'For crying out loud,' he said aloud. 'Stay put!' He removed his shoes and lay down on the bed, half-rising as he realized he'd left all the lights on throughout the house, then falling back with a muttered oath. It was a waste, but he could afford it. If he left the room now he feared he would be flitting about the place for the rest of the night like a lost soul, unable to find peace. 'You don't deserve peace,' he said brutally, thinking of Rich, thousands of miles away, sleeping the sleep of the just, and of Beth, so much closer but infinitely more unreachable. *Beth.* David felt his heart lurch in his chest and he rolled onto his front, trying to smother the pain. 'What have you done?' he said, the words both questioning and condemning. 'What have you done?' He tried to shut down his conscience, which showed him what he did not want to see and painted in sky-high letters the truths he was unwilling to admit.

In desperation, David dug within himself for a shield and something rose up in response, that craven part of him that had gained a foothold in his mind all those months ago. It grew and swelled until all reasoned thoughts fled from the onslaught of pent-up selfishness and desire. Unnoticed, David's hands curled into fists at his sides, ready for battle. He loved Beth. She loved him. She had said so, hadn't she? If Rich had truly loved his wife, he would have stood up to David, refused to leave her. *I would have put her first*, he thought, meanly. *I would put no one above her, now or ever. If he loved her like I do, he would have done the same. She deserves better. She deserves to be with me. Someone who will truly love her, and the child.* His thoughts gathered momentum, fuelled by jealousy and anger, speeding ahead into an alternative future where Beth was his and Rich had never existed. As David lay there, sinking beneath an avalanche of hate, three words fell into his mind, like pebbles lobbed into a raging torrent.

She. Chose. Him.

David didn't know where the words came from, but they rang in his head like a church bell tolling. Then just as abruptly, they were gone, and all other thoughts with them, leaving him empty and numb. After a few moments, David raised his head and fumbled in the inside cover of his childhood Bible. He pulled out two faded snapshots, one of Carlotta, the other of Jonathan.

From childhood, David had always been a popular, outgoing character with a secure sense of self. Perhaps because of this he had rarely formed deep emotional attachments, having no need to do so. When he did, however, he stamped his whole heart on the relationship with a violence of passion that seized hold and never let go. David gazed at the photos, side by side on his pillow. Carlotta and Jonathan, his two great soul mates. And now, rightly or wrongly, there was a third – Beth, whose love had come from nowhere to banish the darkness like a shooting star lighting the night sky. With a wrench, he realized that he had no picture of her. Trapped in the photo, Jonathan smiled out at David, forever 20 in his college scarf and scruffy clothes. David wished his friend were here to advise him, to offer comfort. 'Oh, Jonathan,' he whispered, feeling the old grief as a soldier remembers a lost limb. 'Why didn't you stay? I need you.' Burying his head in his arms, he wept for his losses. For all his heartache over Beth, tonight it was Jonathan's presence he missed the most.

'What happened to him?'

Beth leaned forward in her chair, her curiosity further piqued by the startled glance that passed between Nathan and Jenny. There was a moment's pause, then Jenny said, 'Goodness, that's a question. He died, very tragically.'

'Not long after you left university, Rich said.' Beth shrugged awkwardly. 'Sorry, I'm not trying to be macabre. It's just I thought there was something intriguing about his photo, but I didn't like to ask too much because talking about him made Rich sad.'

'It would do,' Nathan said, quietly. 'Rich was the last person to see Jonathan alive.' He exhaled slowly, gazing into his mug of tea. 'Poor chap.'

'I didn't know.'

'Not the sort of thing Rich would talk about,' Jenny put in with a smile. 'Raw emotion's not really his forte, is it?'

'Remember that time we caught him crying over *Bambi*?' Nathan said.

'You didn't,' Beth giggled.

'Certainly did.'

The mood lightened perceptibly around the table, much to Beth's relief. She passed the cake tin around again. After a moment, Nathan spoke up.

'Jonathan,' he said, 'was what you'd call a character.'

'I know he and David were best friends from way back,' Beth offered.

'Oh, much more than that,' Jenny cut in. 'Like brothers, they were. David owed everything to Jonathan's family.'

'Really?' Beth felt the fatigue falling away from her, revived by the prospect of a window into David's past.

'No question about it,' Nathan continued, lining up a phalanx of shortbread in front of him. 'David came from a very poor family. He was a scholarship boy at boarding school.'

'Did we ever know what happened to his mother?' Jenny murmured, resting her chin on her hand as she tried to recall the details.

'All I know is he was brought up by his dad,' Nathan replied. 'And David didn't go home much. So anyway, David was always David. Good-looking, popular, streetwise, able to look after himself and so on. Once he'd lost his common accent he soon fitted in. But Jonathan had it tough at school. He was –'

'– rather *individual*,' Jenny said. 'He was *different*.'

'He couldn't help it,' said Nathan. 'He misread people, situations. He was vulnerable, and took a bit of flak as a result.'

'Regular beatings is considerably more than a bit of flak, Nathan!' said Jenny.

'Who's telling this story?' Nathan exclaimed.

'Both of us,' Jenny retorted.

'So what happened?' Beth interrupted, completely drawn into the tale.

'It was like this,' Nathan began. 'David went into the common room one day and found a huge crowd in there, all shouting and jeering. When he pushed his way in, he saw Jonathan being virtually strung up by some hulking brute from the sixth form for light entertainment.' Beth began to see where this was going.

'And David stepped in?'

'He did more than that,' chuckled Jenny. 'Told the boy to pick on someone his own size, and then knocked him out cold.'

'Good boxer in his day, David,' Nathan added by way of explanation. 'Very fast.'

'So that's how they became friends,' Beth said, starting to piece it all together.

'That's right,' Jenny said, picking up the story. 'Jonathan invited David home at the end of term, and before long David was spending nearly every holiday there. Jonathan's dad saw David's potential, took him under his wing and got him his first job in Globe Oil.' She dunked her shortbread into her tea. 'And the rest, as they say, is history.'

'It's funny how Nathan, David and Rich all ended up working for the same company, don't you think?' Beth said.

'Looks a bit nepotistic, you mean?' grinned Nathan.

'I know it wasn't,' Beth said, hurriedly. 'Rich was only headhunted from his old company a few years ago.'

'And David had been at Globe for years before Nathan transferred in,' Jenny commented. 'David was the only one who got a leg-up from Jonathan's dad.'

'And why not?' Nathan said affably, leaning back in his chair and stretching his shoulders. An amicable silence fell, during which Beth realized two things. Firstly, that she might fall asleep with her head in the cake tin at any moment and secondly, that her original question had yet to be answered.

'So . . . what did happen to Jonathan?' she asked again. 'In the end?' Nathan and Jenny exchanged a long look. Then Nathan said, choosing his words with care, 'We don't know for sure. Jonathan died in a car accident, but . . .' He tailed off, apparently unwilling to be the one to voice their theory, which Beth guessed was long-held but rarely spoken of.

'The thing is,' Jenny said, swilling the last of her tea round and round in her mug, 'there was something of a question mark over whether it was an accident, or whether Jonathan intended it.' Beth's eyes widened as she interpreted Jenny's meaning. Nathan stared at the table with apparent great interest, examining a knothole in its surface with his thumb. 'Jonathan used to get depressed,' Jenny continued. 'Thought he was a family disappointment. Maybe he was going through one of those times and just couldn't handle it.'

'But he loved David,' Beth said, not wanting to believe in this tragic end. 'He had friends, support.'

'Yes,' agreed Jenny, her head drooping sadly like a wilted flower. 'And David loved Jonathan. But he was recently engaged to Carlotta and busy with his new job . . .' It was her turn to tail off, and Nathan's to fill the breach.

'David would have stopped him,' he said. 'The one person who could have.' He looked up at Beth, his eyes keen, searching. 'If that's what you're asking?' Beth nodded. 'But he didn't know what Jonathan intended,' he explained. 'None of us did. And we never will.'

'He was such a mixture,' Jenny murmured. 'Unpredictable . . . But a very loyal friend.'

'Maybe it *was* an accident,' Beth said, wanting it to be so.

Jenny gave her a wan smile. 'Maybe.'

They stayed as they were for a few moments, each of them motionless, nobody meeting anybody else's eye. A heaviness descended over the room and Beth deeply regretted her insistent curiosity.

'I'm sorry,' she said, awkwardly. 'I've made you sad.'

'Oh, not at all,' said Nathan, squeezing her hand. 'It was a long time ago now.' While this was true, Beth saw that the memory was still a powerful one. Her friends appeared old, their faces slack with melancholy. Faced with such an old, enduring sadness, there was nothing she could say.

Jenny recovered first. 'Well,' she said, briskly, 'we'd better be getting back. The babysitter will think we're engaged in the longest tie-break in the history of badminton.'

'Can we tell her I won?' asked Nathan, hopefully.

'If we must.'

'Excellent.' They left in a flurry of hugs and kisses, the sound of their affectionate bickering fading as they followed the path to the front gate. Beth smiled as she cleared the kitchen table, comforted by the 'realness' of Nathan and Jenny. They were reliably ordinary. Their relationship was like a rock. No, she thought, turning off the lights and feeling her way up the stairs in the dark. Not a rock, which could crumble and erode over time. They were more like trees that swayed and bent with the changes in the wind so that they did not break but kept the essence of what they were, their roots strong and safe beneath the ground. It was a great gift, and surely a God-given one. Wearily, Beth climbed into bed, so tired she did no more than remove her jeans before curling up beneath the duvet. About to turn out the light, she caught sight of her mobile on the floor, poking out of the pocket of her jeans. She really ought to switch it on and check for messages. Cerys might have called, or Rich. Or David. Yawning, Beth leaned over the side of the bed, switched it on and tucked herself back under the covers, the phone in her hand. After several seconds the screen lit up, followed by a short message from Rich.

Strange, really, how a few words can turn the world on its head. In the sliver of time between the end of one breath and the start of the next, everything changed. Hope faded, and Beth knew for certain that now there could be no going back.

Chapter Fifteen

'There must be something we can do.'

'There isn't.'

'Don't say that.'

'Why not? It's the truth.' They were in David's office, he pacing restlessly, she staring out of the window, as though watching their approaching troubles draw nearer with every passing minute. David came to stand beside her and tried to take her hands. She pulled away.

'Beth, don't be like this.'

'Like what?' She turned to him, eyes glittering, her expression cold. 'We have to get real, David. I'm not going to be able to pull this off.'

'Nothing's impossible. And it's not you, it's us,' he replied. 'We can still make this right.'

'Would you listen to yourself?' She gave a high-pitched, hysterical laugh. 'You're not the hero of a Hollywood action film. You're a businessman, a member of the pin-stripe suit and briefcase brigade.' She made it sound like the most worthless occupation in the world. 'You don't rush in and save the world, you just . . .' she paused, searching for something sufficiently insulting, '. . . make transactions.' Her lip curled disdainfully around the word. 'This isn't something you can buy your way out of, David. It's serious.'

'If you've already decided there's nothing I can do, then why are you here?' he challenged, angered by her barbed remarks.

'Because I've got nowhere else to turn, David,' she exclaimed, all but seizing him by the lapels and shaking him, so great was the tide of panic rising inside her. 'I've got no one to talk to.' She strode back and forth in front of him, her breath coming in anguished gasps. 'I can't eat, I can't sleep. If I manage to drop off, I wake up with my jaw clenched so hard my teeth ache. I can't sit down, I can't concentrate, I can't *do anything*.' She stopped, her body shaking with pent-up fear. 'Because whatever I do and wherever I turn, all I see in front of me is my husband's face and the expression on it when I have to tell him the truth.' She wheeled round, pointing her finger at David. 'And I do have to tell him the truth, David. Don't try to pretend otherwise.' David was silent, unable to contradict her. Three more weeks, Rich had said. He needed time to smooth things over, slick a few ruffled feathers back down. 'Three weeks,' Beth said, echoing his thought. 'Nearly a month, David. It's too late.' David stood dumbly before her, arms hanging uselessly at his sides. There were no words of comfort, no neat solution to be devised with a bit of time and clever thinking. They were at a dead end and no amount of remorse, however great, was going to change that.

'Beth, I'm so sorry.' He put a tentative hand on her arm.

She flicked him away like a mosquito. 'You're sorry,' she said, flatly. 'You're sorry, I'm sorry! We're all sorry, but the point is, David, what good does it do us?' She clutched at her head in despair. 'None! None at all.' Beth took a few faltering steps and sank into David's chair, making a Herculean effort to calm down. 'I won't tell him everything,' she said. 'That it was you, I mean.' She turned her face up to him, her expression bleak. 'Bad enough that I . . . that we . . .' she faltered, unable to say it out loud. 'If he knew it was a friend it would be too much to bear.' David watched as she scraped together what meagre strength was left in her. 'I'll be fine,' she claimed. 'I'll go away, find a little place in the country to set up. It'll be OK.'

'But how would you manage?'

'People do.'

'What people?'

'I don't know. Just . . . people.' It was clear that she wasn't thinking straight.

David took a deep breath and put his cards on the table. 'Beth, it's your decision but there is a way out of this. Rather an obvious one. Quick, discreet . . .'

'Despicable?' she cut in.

'Beth, think about it. You can't deny it would solve the immediate problem.'

'So we've done wrong, and the way to right that wrong is by committing another one? The end justifies the means?'

'Sometimes, yes,' he said, levelly.

'David, you can't just . . .' Beth broke off, grappling for the right words, '. . . just take a giant eraser and rub out the consequences of your actions. At any rate, it's not happening, so forget it. I don't want that on my conscience as well.' And so they went on, shooting arguments back and forth amid tears and protestations.

Unaware that Beth was even in the building, Nathan was making his way to David's office. As he approached the door he stopped, seeing it ajar and hearing voices within, David and a woman.

'No. Don't be foolish.'

'If you have a better solution, I'm listening.'

'Let me help you, Beth.' Nathan snatched his hand away from the door as if it had burned him. 'We can sort this out together.'

'I think you've already contributed more than enough. Just leave it.' The sound of footsteps crossing the room. Stepping swiftly forward, Nathan knocked loudly and pushed open the door, almost colliding into Beth as she strode towards him, her face blotched with unhappiness.

'Beth, hi!' He tried for an expression of pleasant surprise. 'How are you?'

'Fine,' she mumbled, brushing past him. 'Sorry, Nathan, I have to go.'

Nathan faced David. 'What's going on?' he said, bluntly. David ran a hand through his hair and let his breath out slowly. 'She's . . . upset.'

'That much was obvious. Why?'

'She wanted me to overrule Rich.' He spread his hands despairingly. 'What can I do, Nathan? Rich is right. We need that gas field to run smoothly, and a stable working environment out there for our staff is vital. Karachaganak is a major investment, you know that.'

'I agree up to a point,' Nathan said cautiously, his brain still trying to make sense of the conversation he'd overheard. What had it meant? 'But if the USA want to smack heads with the Kazakhstani government over *their* projects, that's not really our problem. I think Rich was too quick to get involved. We should stay neutral.'

'Perhaps, but the reality is that anything that affects oil out there affects us. Whether it's on our patch or not.'

Nathan narrowed his eyes, watching his friend closely. What David said added up. Almost. Rich was a tenacious, methodical man and he was a natural mediator with a strong sense of justice. It was no surprise that he had stepped in to try to help, or that he was unwilling to leave without seeing things through to the end. But there was something else that Nathan couldn't put his finger on; something to do with David's swift approval of Rich's choice, a slight tension at the corners of his mouth that implied deceit. It made absolutely no sense, but there it was.

'There's more to this, David,' he said. 'I don't know what, but I see it in your face. What's going on?'

'I'm not at liberty to say,' David replied stiffly, his face impassive.

'Is the whole project under threat out there?'

Inwardly, David breathed a sigh of relief at these words. Nathan was off the scent. More to the point, he'd given David a way out.

'Don't ask me to breach professional confidentiality,' he said. 'You know I can't do that, even for you.'

'Of course not. Sorry to press you on it,' Nathan apologized, immediately dropping the subject. Talk moved on to other things and by the time he left the office, Nathan had all but forgotten the incident. Later he would experience a painful flashback to that conversation and see things all too clearly. But on this particular day he speed-walked happily enough to the Tube amidst a thousand other faceless business suits, his thoughts already on home, Jenny, and a well-earned gin and tonic. David, on the other hand, stayed late at the office, burying himself in work to try to block out his troubles. His subconscious, however, was working furiously on a solution, refusing to accept the role of jilted lover allotted to him by Beth. He was not a good loser, not by any stretch of the imagination. One way or another he always came out on top … Images scrolled through his mind like old-fashioned film reel. Nathan's clear eyes searching him for the truth. Rich, trying to make peace between stubborn men in a turbulent foreign land. Beth, choosing to be humiliated and alone. David's gut clenched. He couldn't allow it to happen. Beth's words returned to him. *The end justifies the means.* 'A turbulent foreign land,' he murmured.

David's hand moved, plucking his phone from the desk, his fingers tapping through the address book until he found the number of an old friend from school days, a wealthy Russian by the name of Ivan. Like with Jonathan, David's friendship had protected short-tempered Ivan from the lavish beatings bestowed on foreign pupils at their school, especially Communists. Where one against ten never prevailed in a fist fight, two did when one of them was David. Now high in the military ranks of his country's army, Ivan would not have forgotten. David punched in the number before he could change his mind.

Exactly two weeks and five days later, Beth was perched on a stool, her elbows propped up on Cerys's industrial kitchen table, watching her sister prepare a batch of scones for the afternoon customers, one cherry, the other cheese.

'You look like a wet weekend,' Cerys remarked, rolling out the cheese mixture with an enormous wooden rolling-pin that reminded Beth of Punch and Judy shows on the beach. She eyed it dubiously.

'That thing makes me nervous,' she replied, avoiding the question.

'Why?'

'I always think you're going to hit someone with it.'

'That's the sort of thing Phoebe would say.' Cerys held the rolling-pin up, examining its potential. 'I suppose it would make a good club,' she said thoughtfully, giving it an experimental swing. She burst out laughing as her sister flinched. 'I can't possibly reach you from here, you wimp. Pass me those cutters, please.' Beth smacked the two fluted steel cutters with the flat of her hand, sending them skidding across the buffed surface like ice hockey pucks. She watched Cerys begin cutting fat rounds. 'When's Phoebe back?' she asked.

'Bedtime,' Cerys said, shortly. 'I think Martin's taking her bowling and then to the cinema.' She shook her head, making the curls bounce. 'Can't believe he's become a McDonald's dad,' she said. 'I thought he was more resourceful. There's so much to do with children round here.'

Beth said nothing, thinking that at least Phoebe had a dad, albeit a rather wet specimen of one. This baby would be completely alone but for her. She touched her stomach surreptitiously. Cerys scraped the remnants of cheese scone mixture together, and threw them down on the table like a challenge.

'What,' she demanded, 'is the matter with you? Rich is home in two days and you look as though you've changed places with me.' It was true. Cerys, managing completely on her own and engaged in various bitter wrangles with Martin over property, money and Phoebe, appeared to be blossoming rather than collapsing beneath the strain. Beth was the one who looked washed-out, depressed and lonely.

Beth fiddled with her hair, avoiding direct eye contact. 'Oh, you know,' she mumbled. 'Just avoiding the housework and stuff. Place is a tip. Lot of work on, too.' In actual fact she had been turning down work, petrified that if she accepted any jobs that meant longer than a day's worth of shots on location her morning sickness would be noticed.

'Come off it, Beth. I –' Cerys broke off as Katie, one of the new Saturday staff she'd taken on, stuck her head in from the shop. 'OK, Katie?' Beth jumped, startled by the contrast between the girl's tiny frame and the mass of fat black dreadlocks sprouting from her head, randomly studded with scraps of ribbon, lace and hair slides. She looked like Medusa after a brawl at the hairdresser's.

'All under control,' beamed Katie, enviably fresh-faced and keen. 'Do you need a hand with anything?'

'All under control, thanks. Scones ready to go in half an hour.'

'OK, boss.' She disappeared back into the shop with a cheery wave.

'What on earth,' said Beth, raising her eyebrows, 'was that?'

'That's Katie,' Cerys shrugged, flouring the table for the cherry scone mixture. 'Hard worker, very resourceful. The shock value wears off after a couple of days. Phoebe thinks she's hilarious.'

'Health and safety?'

'She ties it back and wears the hat,' Cerys grinned. 'I keep her away from the ovens and any naked flames, just in case.'

She picked up the rolling-pin and gave Beth a stern look. 'You're a terrible liar, Beth. Something's been eating away at you for weeks now, and you think you've been so clever, hiding it so as not to bother anybody.' She pummelled the mixture with her rolling-pin and reached for the cutters. 'You look like death warmed up, and Jenny said as much to me after she saw you lately. Mum thinks you *are* dying, if you want to know.'

'Mum thinks we're dying if we sneeze twice in a row.'

'Granted, but it's not fair of you to let her worry like that. She'll make herself ill at this rate and then we'll all get it in the neck. Now, what's with the condemned woman routine?'

'Cerys, leave me be,' Beth pleaded, scrabbling in her bag as her phone started to ring.

'I will *not* leave you be. Whatever's wrong, you'll feel much better once you've got it off your chest. Take it from someone who knows,' Cerys grimaced. 'And don't tell me you came down here for the day just to sit and watch me bake.' Suddenly she dashed round the table and snatched the phone from Beth's hand before she could answer it.

'Give it back, it might be Rich!' Cerys glanced at the display.

'It is.' She stepped out of range as Beth swiped at her arm.

'Give it *back*!'

'Not until you tell me.'

'Cerys!'

'No. Tell, tell, tell, tell, tell, tell, TELL.'

Beth was at the end of her tether. 'Alright! I'm pregnant!' she yelled, jumping up and seizing the phone from her sister's hand. 'Pregnant. Satisfied?' She turned her back on Cerys's stupefied face and answered the phone.

'Hello?'

'Hi, darling,' said Rich jovially. 'Only forty-eight hours to go, I'm counting down.'

'Me too,' said Beth, her voice almost cracking.

'I can't win with you,' he teased. 'You cry when I go, you cry when I'm away, and now you cry when I'm coming home. You must have cried enough to fill a swimming pool by now.'

'At least,' Beth said, weakly. 'Probably a couple of baths as well.'

Rich laughed, his voice brimming with happiness. 'I love you so much, Beth. I can't wait to get back to you.'

'Me too.' Behind her, Cerys was loading the scones onto baking trays, feeding them to the oven with trembling hands. 'Remind me what time your flight gets in?'

'Seven-thirty in the evening,' he replied. 'You going to pick me up?'

'Of course.'

'I'm in the middle of packing now,' Rich said, looking at the messy contents of his suitcase.

'How's it going?'

'Well, I reckon there's not much point folding anything when it's going straight in the wash, so it's going fine,' he replied, smiling as Beth groaned in despair. 'Just a second, there's someone at the door.' He crossed the room and pulled the door open to reveal a stranger in a charcoal grey suit standing outside, hands resting casually in his jacket pockets. 'Can I help you?' he asked in a polite, clear voice, hoping the man had some English. Meanwhile, Beth was watching her sister out of the corner of her eye, knowing the end of the phone call would signal interrogation and the beginning of the end of her happy, cosy life. She wished Rich would go on talking forever so the moment would never come. Without warning there was a loud bang in her ear, followed by a crash, the sound of a phone being dropped. Reflexively, Beth held the phone away from her ear, waited a few seconds to give him time to pick up on his end, then spoke again.

'Rich? Are you there, Rich?'

Nothing.

'Hello? Rich?' A quick glance at the phone showed that they hadn't been cut off, but there was no response whatsoever.

'Rich?' She was panicking now. Had that noise been the door banging shut? Had Rich fallen somehow and knocked himself out? Sensing trouble, Cerys was immediately at her side. 'What –'

'Shut up.' Straining, Beth thought she'd heard her name spoken faintly, but Cerys had talked over it and now there was nothing. 'Rich, don't mess about. Are you OK?' Abruptly she ended the call. The sisters looked at each other, the reasons for their white, shocked faces different, but their expressions the same. 'Something's wrong,' Beth said.

'You bet it is.'

'No. Listen, will you? Something's wrong with Rich.'

'So call him back.'

So it was that the last sound Richard Hampton ever heard as he lay in pooling blood from a single gunshot wound to the heart, on the floor of a rented apartment thousands of miles from home, was the urgent bleep of a mobile phone lying just out of reach.

Chapter Sixteen

'Are you awake, Jen?' There was a muffled groan beside him in the dark.

'Yeah. You?'

'No, I'm talking in my sleep. Oof.' Nathan gasped as a pillow struck his face. Jenny sat up and snapped the light on.

'You asked for that,' she said tersely, swinging her legs out of bed and pushing her feet into her slippers. 'This is no time to be facetious. I'm making a cup of tea. Do you want one?'

'Yes, please.' Nathan struggled up in bed, his eyes hot and prickly from hours of staring at nothing. 'I'll come, too.'

'Alright. Bring the baby monitor, then.' Together they tiptoed downstairs and regrouped in the kitchen, Nathan having stopped en route to switch the central heating on despite hissed protests from Jenny that it was almost summer.

'Makes no difference,' he said, grumpily. 'It's Baltic in here.'

'Come and stand by the kettle, then.'

'Very funny.' But he did as he was told, wrapping his arms tightly around her from behind as she fussed with mugs and tea bags, yawning.

'What's keeping you awake?' she asked.

'Same thing as you, I expect.'

'Beth?'

'No, Rich, actually.' He rested his chin on her head and exhaled heavily. 'It's been a bit of a day, hasn't it?'

'That's the understatement of the century,' she said. 'Might as well make a pot. Budge over, I need to get to the milk.' Nathan fetched a packet of biscuits and they sat side by side at the kitchen table with the teapot between them, huddled wordlessly over their mugs as if they were brewing up magic potions that could turn back the clock and make everything right.

'It's a bad business,' Nathan said at last.

'Jammie Dodger?'

'Might as well.' In the grand scheme of things, dieting wasn't much of a priority at the moment. Rich's funeral had taken place earlier that day at Holy Trinity in Thames Ditton, his former parish church. Standing room only. After weeks of waiting, the body had at last been flown home after significant pressure from Globe Oil. No firm conclusions had been reached by the Kazakhstani authorities concerning Mr Hampton's murder. In fact, the best they had been able to come up with so far was a case of mistaken identity. Globe representatives had blamed the rising tensions between the American and Kazakhstani oilfield operators, and implied that Rich had been targeted by someone who didn't want to see those tensions resolved. The authorities had responded with the very reasonable point that Rich had been about to depart for home and had no intention of further involvement. Anyone wanting him out of the way, they argued, would have achieved their aim simply by letting him go. There was no need to kill him. Besides which, he was well-liked by both groups. Mistaken identity, they said, was surprisingly common in the shady political underworld. All it took was a simple mistake in a scribbled address, one wrong digit. It happened, they said, from time to time. A deranged attacker was another theory, either mentally disturbed or under the influence of drugs. This, too, had been tragically known to happen. Naturally, they would continue to investigate, but . . .

'No witnesses, no fingerprints, no clear motive,' Nathan murmured, remembering the report that Globe Oil had received. 'I just can't believe it.'

'I know. But it's Beth I can't get my head round. Look what Rich would have come home to. An unfaithful wife and a cuckoo in the nest.'

'You can't say he's better off dead, love.'

'No,' she agreed, rubbing her eyes, sore from too much crying and the effort of alternately releasing and containing her grief depending on whether the children were around. 'I'm not saying that, of course I'm not.'

'Perhaps she was hoping to get away with it,' Nathan offered, hating the suggestion even as he made it.

'Impossible,' Jenny replied, topping up their mugs from the pot. 'Cerys said she's somewhere between sixteen and twenty weeks.'

'And she won't say who the father is?'

'Nope. All she would tell Cerys is that she'd made a stupid mistake and that it was all over. Her intention was to tell Rich the minute he got home, and then leave and raise the baby on her own. Very laudable, I'm sure,' she sniffed.

'At least she's keeping the baby.'

'Don't defend her, Nathan,' snapped Jenny.

'I'm not. I'm just saying she could have taken the easy way out. There's a certain amount of integrity in her.'

'Mmph.' Jenny clearly wasn't impressed. 'My view is that she was banking on Rich forgiving her.'

'I don't think so,' Nathan said, taking his fifth biscuit. 'Whatever else she might be, Beth's a realist. She's certainly punishing herself now. You saw her today, Jen. She did love him.'

'I know.' Seeing her close to tears again, Nathan slid closer and put his arm around her shoulders. 'I don't hate her or anything,' Jenny said. 'I'm sorry for her. Nobody's perfect and all that. I just feel a bit – betrayed, somehow. As a friend.' She looked up at him. 'Does that sound stupid?'

'No,' said Nathan. 'I do too. And Cerys is beside herself, by all accounts.'

'Yes,' Jenny grimaced. 'It's all a bit near the knuckle, I think.'

'She's standing by her sister, though, surely?'

'Of course. But things are a little . . . strained, I'd say.' She snuggled closer, taking comfort from Nathan's solid presence. 'I'm meeting her and Phoebe tomorrow.'

'She's not with Beth?'

'Apparently Beth wants to be on her own.' Jenny caught sight of the kitchen clock and groaned. 'It's half past three, Nathan. The kids will be up in a few hours and we've got church at 9:30. Let's try to get some sleep.'

'You're the boss.' Nathan pulled Jenny to her feet and held her close for a long moment without speaking. Then they made their way back to bed, Nathan's unvoiced suspicion weighing him down. After a further half an hour of mutual ceiling-gazing, Nathan gave in. He had tried everything to quell his fear, and the desperate prayers he eventually resorted to resulted in an alarming certainty that his suspicion was correct. That snippet of overheard conversation between David and Beth refused to go away. He felt as though he had a pressure cooker in his chest.

'Jenny?'

'Yes?'

'Beth's baby.'

'What about it?'

'I think David's the father.'

'You what?' In a heartbeat the light was on, and they were facing each other wide-eyed across the duvet.

'It's just a suspicion, but . . .' It was as if hearing the words aloud had released something in Nathan's head, because the connections were sparking thick and fast now, his memory scouring the past five months with alarming precision. A look here, a comment there. That trip to the Albert Hall. Hadn't David seemed much brighter, more hopeful in recent months? All of it could be justified or explained away, but somehow Nathan knew he was staring at the truth, or some part of it. Behind everything towered the old, warning image that had come to him so many months ago. David and the house of cards. Jenny shook her head, unable to take it in.

'How can you be so sure?'

'Because it's ugly and I want it to go away, but it won't.'

Jenny sat back against the headboard, her eyes focused on her husband's face.

'From the beginning, Nathan,' she ordered. 'And don't leave a single thing out.'

Neither of them got any sleep that night.

'Can you believe it?' Cerys thrust the Sunday paper under Jenny's nose. 'I mean, can you *actually* believe it? I can't believe it.' She flung herself down on the park bench and stared moodily at the playground sandpit, where Phoebe was playing diggers with Abigail and Michael. Beside them, Rory was printing his hands into the sand and licking his palms with solemn concentration.

'Cerys, calm down,' Jenny began. 'I've no idea what you're talking about.'

'Read it and you'll see.' Cerys jabbed her finger at the popular broadsheet now in Jenny's fist. 'Page five.'

'Hold this.' Jenny passed her cardboard coffee cup and leafed through the crumpled pages, shading her eyes from the sun. It was 11:30 and already too warm for her liking. 'Oh,' she said, seeing a picture of Beth at Rich's graveside, flanked by Nathan and David, each of them holding her arms for support. The caption above it read 'Globe Oil Widow Mourns Murdered Husband'. 'OK,' she said. 'Well, it was bound to be reported in the press, and . . . oh. Oh.'

'Yes,' said Cerys. 'Oh.' Leaning across, she read aloud from the page. '*Grieving widow Elizabeth Hampton spent just one short visit with her husband during his posting to Globe Oil's newly constructed oilfield in Kazakhstan, flying out to join him over the Christmas period. Now several months pregnant and newly widowed, she is faced with an uncertain future alone. They had been married just two years. David Samuel, chairman of Globe Oil and a close friend of the Hamptons, has pledged the support of Globe Oil to Mrs Hampton and her unborn child and has promised to pursue the investigation of Mr Hampton's murder until the truth is uncovered.*' She shook her head angrily. 'Why are they protecting Beth?'

'Er, who?' asked Jenny, cautiously.

'Globe Oil, who else?' Cerys said.

'I assume they're doing it for Rich,' Jenny pointed out calmly. 'So that he's remembered for himself and not for . . . anything else,' she finished. 'Very few people would know that Beth hadn't visited Rich, and those that do probably respect him enough to keep their mouths shut. He was well-liked.' She laid a hand on the distraught woman's arm. 'Listen, surely you don't want your own sister hounded and disgraced by the press?' she said, gently.

Cerys took a deep, shuddering breath, staring down at her hands. 'No,' she admitted. 'I don't.' She looked up, meeting Jenny's sympathetic gaze. 'I think I'm finding it all a bit difficult, with my own problems – a bit close to home. It's hard to find my own sister on the opposite side of the fence, you know?' She looked away, her eyes seeking out Phoebe in the sandpit. 'Harder to hate Martin for what he did to us, if that makes any sense at all.'

Jenny squeezed Cerys's hand. 'It makes perfect sense,' she said. 'And I think you're doing the right thing, sticking by Beth. Life is going to be hard enough for her now as it is.' Especially with David hounding her, she thought, judging it best not to reveal any of the sordid possibilities she and Nathan had shared last night. 'Troubles come and go, but family is forever,' she said, aloud. Cerys nodded her agreement.

'You look shattered, by the way,' Cerys said.

'I am. The kids were up early again,' Jenny fibbed. 'And we had Messy Church this morning, which is always a bit of a circus.'

'I did wonder why you've got blue paint in your hair.'

'All for a good cause.'

Cerys stood up and dusted herself down. 'Sit here and drink your coffee,' she ordered. 'And then get another one from the kiosk.'

'You're just as tired as I am,' Jenny objected.

Cerys brushed her protests away. 'Nah. I can't give you a whole day of rest, but I can do a stint in the sandpit.' She strolled off, calling to the children and leaving Jenny to reflect on an unusual blessing. If it weren't for the children they would probably be holed up somewhere, nursing their shared grief and railing at the heavens. As it was, they had to get straight up and carry on, packing their sorrow for the onward journey. This way, they could bear a small dose every day, like medicine, until eventually it was gone and they were healed. While it felt odd to be out and about living a normal life, it was, she decided, no bad thing. Glancing at her watch, she saw that it was almost noon. Nathan would be there by now. She closed her eyes and sent up a prayer for strength.

Opening his eyes, Nathan sucked in a deep breath, squared his shoulders and rang the bell. Standing on the doorstep of David's imposing home, he felt suddenly small and insignificant. He told himself not to be an idiot. This was David, his old friend. There was nothing to be afraid of. But standing there, Nathan realized he was afraid – very afraid. He wanted to be told that he was a fool, upbraided for his suspicions, berated for daring to think so badly of such a good man. He wanted to be sent packing, embarrassed and remorseful. He wanted to be begging David's pardon for his outrageous, unfounded accusations, and promising to make it up to him.

As he waited, adrenalin fizzing in his veins, something told him it wasn't going to be that way. Once that door opened he was committed to this path, no going back. Still he waited, heart hammering in his chest. It crossed his mind that there was still time to leave, nip round the corner to where the car was parked and get away, leave well alone. Least said, soonest mended. 'You can't do that, Nathan,' he told himself sternly. 'Rich was your friend, too.' With that, the door swung inwards and there was David, smart and sober in jeans and a black V-necked jumper, a surprised smile on his face.

'Nathan,' he said. 'Come in, mate, come in.'

'Thanks.' Nathan followed him into the house and down the hallway to the kitchen, staring at David's back and thinking that there'd been no hesitation in the invitation, not for a second. What if he was wrong? Was it really worth risking a friendship over one lousy suspicion? *Let it go, Nathan. Let it go. It's not your business.* He clutched at his courage with sweating hands.

'Just putting some coffee on,' David said, indicating the half-filled cafetiere on the polished worktop. *You must do this, Nathan.* With a start, Nathan realized that David was staring expectantly at him.

'What?'

'I said, do you want one?'

'Oh.' Nathan stuffed his hands in his pockets. 'Yes, great.'

'There's tea if you'd rather.'

'No, coffee's great, thanks.' The radio twittered in the background, a female presenter gravely relaying the latest in celebrity gossip as though it were gospel truth. David eased himself onto a chrome, leather-cushioned stool at the breakfast bar, and gestured at its twin. Nathan sat.

'So,' said David, easing the plunger down on the cafetiere. 'Trouble?' When Nathan said nothing he went on. 'You saw the papers?'

'I saw them, yes. Was it your idea, the cover story?'

'Yeah.' David passed a hand over his face. 'When Beth told me her news I knew something would be needed.'

'Quick thinking.'

'Well, I had several weeks to consider it.' *And you already knew.* Nathan pulled his coffee cup towards him and took a swig. 'David,' he began carefully, inching his way into the conversation like a man in the dark. 'I need to ask you something.'

'Sure, fire away.'

'If you knew, or – or you were pretty sure that a friend had done wrong, would you challenge them, or would you let it go?'

'What kind of wrong are we talking about here? Serious wrong or accepting too much change in the supermarket type of wrong?'

'Serious,' Nathan said, beginning to see how the conversation might play out. 'Something morally wrong.'

'A good friend?' David asked, his clear eyes on Nathan's troubled face.

'Close, yes.' David's forehead furrowed in thought, his white china cup cradled between his palms. 'Judging from the look on your face, I'd say this was a big deal,' he commented. 'So, yes. I would challenge a friend if they'd done something that was gravely, morally wrong. Three reasons.'

He added more sugar to his coffee, the rhythmic clink of the spoon grating on Nathan's taut nerves. 'One, because it's the just thing to do. Two, for the sake of your own integrity. Three, for your friend's sake. One day they might even thank you for it.' He smiled at Nathan. 'I don't want to pry, but is it really such a terrible thing? I've never seen you so uptight.'

'Adultery,' Nathan mumbled indistinctly, barely able to get the word out. David's face darkened. 'Then don't hesitate, Nathan,' he advised. 'Speak out, and the sooner the better. There might still be time to set matters right.'

It was now or never.

'David?'

'Yes, Nathan.'

'The friend is you.'

'Pardon?'

'It's you, David.' Nathan plunged on, knowing that he had to keep going now that he'd begun. 'I know. I know about you and Beth. I know all of it.' David froze, his hands still gripping the cup in midair.

'How?'

'I worked it out, David. I'm not a fool.' Nathan felt anger burning through him, bringing courage with it. 'How could you do it, David?' he demanded, seeming to grow in stature with every word. 'Rich was your friend, your good friend. He trusted you.' The colour drained from David's face, and he hunched in on himself like a defenceless creature retreating into its shell.

'I didn't mean it,' he whispered, his eyes begging Nathan for forgiveness, understanding, anything but this pitiless judgement from his friend.

'You had a wife, and a beautiful daughter,' Nathan thundered. 'You had many happy years together. She was taken from you so you thought you'd steal someone else's, is that it? What you'd been given wasn't enough?'

'No, I didn't think . . . I didn't mean . . .'

'No good will come of this, David,' Nathan warned him. 'Believe me.'

'I'm sorry.' David was prone on the breakfast bar, his head buried in his arms.

'Who are you apologizing to? Your friend is *dead*.' Nathan paused, his breathing harsh and rapid.

'I will make amends, Nathan,' David whispered. 'I swear to you.'

'David the Golden Boy, David the charmer,' Nathan spat scathingly. 'David the winner. No one gets the better of David Samuel, eh?' New knowledge came to him as he stood there, watching his friend collapse beneath the guilt heaped on him like rocks. Nathan made the final accusation. 'I can't prove it,' he said, his voice low but full of strength. 'But I know in my heart, David, that you had something to do with Rich's death.'

'No,' David wept. 'You can't know such a thing.'

'You're right, I can't! But I can feel it. I know you, David, and I say that you wanted Beth for yourself. Tell me why you tried to call Rich home.'

David shook his head, beyond speech.

'You were trying to cover up your affair! And when that didn't work, Beth decided to face up to Rich alone, didn't she? Didn't she?' he roared. 'I overheard you talking, David, so don't lie to me. It all makes sense now.'

'Yes,' David admitted, his shoulders shaking.

'And you couldn't stand that, could you,' Nathan said in disgust. 'You couldn't stand being the loser, and you disguised your selfishness as a noble act to save Beth's honour.' David made no reply. 'I'm not saying you pulled the trigger. But his death suited your purposes, and I say you had a hand in it somehow.' His mind was clear now, his hands steady as he stood up. 'And even if you didn't,' he went on, 'the outcome gives you everything you wanted.'

'I loved him too,' David said, pathetically.

'No, David.' Nathan turned and walked to the door. 'You love yourself. What were you planning? To wait a few months and then develop a "new friendship" with the grieving widow? Magnanimously take on the child as your own?' David flinched. This was exactly what he had intended, but in Nathan's mouth the words had the invidious ring of treachery. He saw himself through Nathan's eyes – dishonest, self-serving and wicked. Nathan grasped the door handle and glanced back. 'This stays between us,' he said, shortly. 'I give you that much, for friendship's sake. But I found you out, and nothing stays hidden forever.'

David stared helplessly at him. 'And Beth?' he whispered. 'You won't tell her?'

'Like I said, I can't prove anything,' Nathan repeated. 'Nobody gets convicted on a hunch. What you do about it is on your conscience, not mine.'

'She'd never forgive me –'

'It's not Beth's forgiveness I'd be worrying about, if I were you. One day you'll be held to account for this by a much higher authority.' Nathan opened the door and stepped into the hall. 'We reap what we sow, David. You remember that.'

'Beth, I'm not sure this is a terribly good idea.' Janet hovered at the bedroom door, looking on as Beth crammed a few final items into her suitcase. 'Quite apart from anything else, I don't think you ought to be carrying that in your condition.'

'I'll tow it,' Beth said, numbly. She zipped the case shut and sat down on the bed, her favourite camera packed ready in its own holdall. 'Please, Janet,' she said, her hands open in supplication. 'I need to get away for a while, clear my head. I don't want to be . . . bothered by anybody.' She meant David, but Janet interpreted this to mean the world at large. 'Well, I can understand that,' she said, uncertainly. 'When my husband died, I got sick of people calling and dropping by to check on me as though I'd suddenly lost all my faculties. But your family, you know –' She broke off for a second, remembering. 'Though come to think of it, they were the worst of all,' she said, ruefully. 'I damn-near brained my sister with a saucepan when she asked if I felt up to making a boiled egg six weeks after the funeral.' Beth giggled despite herself. It was either that or cry.

'I want to get right away for a while,' she said, trying to explain. 'While I can still fly.' She touched her stomach, which had the beginnings of a gentle swell beneath her top. 'And I want to see the project through,' she added. 'It was my idea.'

'Ye-es,' Janet agreed. 'I see that. Well, let's proceed as planned.'

'Who was it that said when you're feeling as bad as you think you can possibly feel, you should go out and do something for those worse off than yourself?' Beth asked as together they lugged her bags downstairs and out to Janet's waiting car. 'Or words to that effect.'

'Ghandi?' guessed Janet, wheezing with exertion. 'Mother Teresa?'

'Yes, her,' Beth said, seizing on the name. 'That sums up how I feel exactly.'

'Well, good for you,' said Janet, slamming the boot of her Micra and sliding into the driver's seat. 'Heathrow it is, then. Sure you've got everything?'

Beth did a quick mental inventory. Luggage, broken heart, passport, guilty conscience, camera, and somebody else's child. 'Yep,' she said. 'Everything and more.' I'll call Cerys when I get there, she promised herself, already fearing the call. Better that than have her mother barricade the terminal at the airport. It was just as likely that they'd yell good riddance and shake her dust off their heels, she thought glumly as the car pulled away. Either way, she'd be long gone by the time they knew.

'Uganda, here I come.'

Chapter Seventeen

African Time

'Jambo mzungu!'

  'Mzungu, how are you?'

  'Mzungu, mzungu!'

Beth felt her face break into a smile. Letting go of her broad-brimmed grey hat for a second, she risked a quick wave at the excited children from her perch on the back of a battered moped, or *Boda-boda* as the locals called them. It was the quickest way to get around, though admittedly not all that safe. However, Beth wasn't doing 'safe' just now. *Jambo mzungu* meant 'Hello, white person,' and the children of Lira and its outlying villages found Beth, with her blonde hair, pale skin and outlandish trousers, a figure of great curiosity.

After another long day out in the local countryside, photographing some families who grew the sunflower and rice crops common in the northern regions of Uganda, Beth was tired but exhilarated and looking forward to home. For the last three weeks, this had been a small room in the annexe at the rear of Nightingale's school in the city of Lira, where some of the staff had quarters. Beth couldn't wait to get back and review the photos on her laptop. She had taken some wonderful shots of young children standing amid the burgeoning sunflowers, their smiles as bright as the yellow-headed plants, for all their hardship. The moped steered along the wide road which felt both city-like and rural, with rust-red earth either side of the hard surface instead of pavements, and a triangular red-rimmed street sign growing from the earth at a jaunty angle, like the trees opposite it. Also, there were pedestrians on the road, walking with the fluid, stately grace that Beth had come to associate with these beautiful African people since her arrival at Entebbe airport three weeks ago. Wherever they were going, their movements seemed to say they would arrive at their destinations in good time – good time meaning whatever the time was when they got there. African time was the antithesis of Western punctuality, and Beth loved it.

Peering past the driver, she saw the Nightingale school up ahead and was ready when they came to a juddering stop by the front entrance. The driver switched the engine off and turned to look at his precious cargo. 'Please, *Nyabo*,' he said, reproachfully. 'Do not wave so much. You must hold on. My wife will not be pleased if she discovers you lying in the road.' Beth dismounted with some difficulty and arranged a contrite look on her face.

'I apologize, Munyiga Christopher,' she said, solemnly. 'And please, call me Beth.' Her companion nodded politely. Then their faces broke into identical smiles. This exchange had become a daily ritual between them, each knowing full well the offences would be committed again tomorrow. Just as Beth would continue to wave at the children when she ought to be holding onto the bike, so Munyiga would call her *Nyaba*, 'Madam,' with quiet, persistent dignity. At least he didn't kneel and grasp her hand as the older women did in the villages they visited, a gesture that Beth found uncomfortable and profoundly humbling.

Moments later, a second moped chugged into view and drew up behind them. A small Ugandan woman leaped off the back and hurried over, her simple white T-shirt tucked neatly into her bright orange skirt flapping in the breeze. She was Abbo Maria, Munyiga Christopher's wife and Beth's guide. 'You took good care on the road, Munyiga?' she demanded.

'I did, Abbo,' he responded, his toothy smile full of warmth. 'As you see.'

Abbo Maria took Beth's hand. 'Come,' she smiled. 'It is time to eat. Then, if you are not too tired, I think the girls will do some paper beading work tonight if you would like to join them.'

'Thank you, I'd like that,' Beth replied, delighted at the chance of completing the delicate bracelet of paper beads she had been making under the tuition of the female staff. 'And I'm not at all tired.' Abbo Maria shook her head in gentle disbelief and led Beth inside.

The school was a long, low building made of ochre-coloured stone, a single broad white strip running the length of the front façade above the double-fronted windows spaced at regular intervals. For the most part the roof was flat, but the main entrance sported a private sloped roof like a Chinese hat. Inside, the classrooms and offices were cool, clean and, above all, welcoming.

In the small whitewashed refectory, Beth took her evening meal at one of the long trestle tables, flanked by

Abbo Maria, Munyiga Christopher and half a dozen of the staff, a mixture of teachers and health workers. Abbo Maria and her husband, Munyiga Christopher, worked jointly as project directors, managing their Ugandan staff, foreign volunteers, and liaising with their funding partners in the UK. It was an enormous task and one which they approached with tremendous energy and commitment. Dinner was *luwombo*, a groundnut sauce steamed in banana leaves and served with 'food', which is what the Ugandans called any carbohydrate. Tonight it was rice, and Beth noted with the usual flush of shame that hers was the only meal to which meat had been added. She bitterly regretted informing the staff of her pregnancy. Had it been left to her, she would have kept quiet, reckoning her small five-month bump would pass unnoticed, but Janet had interfered, phoning ahead to make sure Nightingale school was fully aware, and to check that provisions could be made. As far as Beth could make out, 'provisions' meant feeding her twice as much as anyone else and preventing her from doing anything remotely dangerous. She tried to accept this with good grace, knowing that Abbo Maria and Munyiga Christopher were responsible for her care, but some of the restrictions chafed. Abbo Maria had strictly forbidden overnight stays in any of the villages, despite Beth's pleas to be permitted to see more of the area. 'We cannot risk malaria for you and your child,' she had said to a crestfallen Beth, though not unkindly.

'But I have medication,' Beth had protested, producing the chloroquine tablets the doctor had reluctantly prescribed for her. Persuading him had not been easy but pressing ahead with the long-planned trip to Uganda had kept Beth going during the weeks of waiting for Rich to be brought home. Utterly determined, she had steamrollered the beleaguered GP into submission with a cock-and-bull tale. In hindsight, she wasn't quite sure whether he had believed her claims to have elderly missionary parents in Uganda, but he had handed over the prescription in the end. Abbo Maria, however, was impossible to steamroller into anything, and had remained implacable on the subject in a most irritatingly caring way.

'Nothing,' she said firmly, 'matters more in the world than a child. There is no greater gift.' Beth had bowed her head, the words an unintentional rebuke to her own mixed feelings about the baby.

Also at the table were two other volunteers, a musician called Bryan Topps and an artist named DeeDee Rose, both on six-month teaching sabbaticals. Crucially for Beth, they had been relatively cut off from the British press, for which she was intensely thankful. DeeDee gave her a little wave from across the table, her dark hair pulled into rough pigtails which looked rather misplaced on a woman in her forties. 'Good shooting today?' she asked, as if Beth had been out hunting lions.

'Yes, brilliant,' Beth said, briefly describing the sunflower fields, and picking out the high points of the day.

'Sounds great,' said DeeDee, pushing her glasses up her nose in a habitual gesture that sent the Nightingale children into hysterics, though none of them seemed able to say why.

'Sorry I missed choir practise,' Beth apologized. 'We got caught up talking.' At the start and end of every school day, the entire community of staff and pupils gathered in front of the building for singing, or in the refectory during the rainy season. Often they drew an appreciative crowd of passing locals. Their natural musicality was astonishing, and the rhythmic, earthy harmonies made Beth's spine tingle.

'It's a big part of our culture – of all African cultures,' Abbo Maria had said modestly in response to Beth's effusive praise. It was impossible to stand still when the Nightingales sang, and during one of their morning choir practises Beth had felt the baby kick for the first time, dancing to the heart-beat of Africa. Choir practise was the best part of Beth's day, and she was genuinely sorry to have missed it.

'Hey, no problem,' DeeDee smiled. 'There's always tomorrow.'

'I'll be there,' Beth assured her. 'Tomorrow is my last day.'

'I'd completely forgotten,' DeeDee said, clapping a hand to her mouth. 'Where did the last three weeks go?'

'Tell me about it.'

'You can't stay longer?'

'No, there are restrictions on pregnant women flying,' Beth said, patting her stomach. By the time they had travelled back to Kampala, then on to Entebbe airport, and from there to Heathrow, another week would have gone by, and Beth would be six months pregnant.

'We will miss you,' said Masani Catherine, a petite, bright-eyed young nurse who ducked her head shyly as she cleared Beth's plate.

'Will you help me finish my bracelet tonight?' Beth asked. 'If you aren't too busy?'

'Masani is never too busy to talk,' joked Ojore Thomas, an English teacher whose eyes were crinkled at the corners from a lifetime of smiling, and whose deep, rolling laugh could shake the walls.

'Ha,' said Masani, wagging a fork at him. 'But the difference between us, Ojore, is that while women are talking, their fingers are working and making good use of the time. When you men are flapping your mouths you are capable of doing nothing else.' The refectory erupted in peals of good-natured laughter, and Beth felt hot tears well up at the thought of leaving the Nightingale school, with all its love and camaraderie in the face of such great odds. There was a resilience about the staff, an ability to take almost any circumstance, find the good in it, no matter how small, and build upwards from there. It was a timely lesson.

An hour later, the women convened in one of the classrooms, bringing their beadwork with them. Beth sat between Masani Catherine and Kissa Grace, concentrating on the close work as the others chatted and laughed companionably. They were all proficient in making the paper bead jewellery that was popular with Fair Trade businesses which sold the pieces all over the world. They were made from coloured paper, usually magazines, by winding thin strips round needles to form a bead. This done, they were steeped in cleaning fluid, dried and lacquered. Beth had completed a short necklace, and was now working on a bracelet. It was fiddly work and from time to time, one of the women would break off without fuss and move Beth's hand just so, or take a strip of paper from her and demonstrate the correct technique for winding it onto the needle. It was some time before Beth gathered the courage to ask the question she had wanted to ask for a long time.

'Abbo Maria,' she began tentatively. 'May I ask you something?'

'Of course.' The conversation stilled, all eyes turning to Beth.

'How long will it be, in your opinion, until Uganda recovers from these years of violence?' she asked. 'Although this is my first visit to Lira, it is my fourth visit to Uganda and I have never yet dared to ask.' A murmur ran around the circle, but it was left to Abbo Maria to respond. She considered for a long time, her head on one side, before giving her reply.

'North of here, in Gulu,' she began, 'the IDP camps for internally displaced people have begun to close, which is both good and bad. Then, there are many non-government organizations and charities working to support the damaged people of northern Uganda ... Schools like ours, projects which work to reunite families, projects which work to create new families from orphans of war, people willing to educate and train others in the art of peace, not war.' She paused, acknowledging the nods of agreement from her companions, her expression solemn. 'Still, it will be many years, I believe many lifetimes, until the wounds gouged by Joseph Kony and the LRA into the heart of Uganda will scar over and heal. But the work we do now is undoubtedly changing lives. With God's grace, it will also change the lives of people yet to be.' There was a chorus of approval from the assembled women.

'I will do everything I can to help you,' Beth promised, feeling small and insignificant in the face of their courage. 'Always.'

'With your clever camera and your English Nightingale partners, you will,' agreed Masani Catherine. 'But not,' she added with gentle humour, 'through your beadwork, I think.' Beth looked down in embarrassment at the messy, mismatched beads in her lap and for the second time that evening, laughter shook the air.

As she lay in bed that night, Beth took long, deep breaths, trying to draw into herself all that was good about Uganda, and carry it home. At the foot of her bed, she could just make out the shape of the plain wooden cross on the wall. Uganda was staunchly and unashamedly religious, the doors of even the humblest dwellings chalked with words of blessing and welcome to all who entered. Beth had grown used to the frequent mention of God and his Providence during her stay, and even found it comforting at times, though she was unsure of her own views on the matter.

'What do you think about all this?' she mumbled, addressing the silent cross. 'If you're even there at all.' Assuming God was there and paying any attention, surely he approved of the restorative work in Uganda, Beth mused, rolling onto her side as sleep drew near. What he might think of her own life was something she preferred not to consider.

The next morning, a car arrived to drive her back through the beautiful Ugandan countryside, past Jinja and Kampala, all the way to Lake Victoria and Entebbe. As she stood beside the car, waiting to make her farewells, the Nightingale community filed out of the main entrance and formed into ranks with DeeDee at their head. 'Couldn't let you go without a song,' she grinned. One by one the staff came forward to say goodbye, and Masani Catherine pressed two bracelets into Beth's hand, one a perfect miniature made of the tiniest beads.

'For your child,' she said. 'If it is a daughter, you must name her Nabulungi. It means beautiful.'

Last of all were Abbo Maria and Munyiga Christopher, Abbo sinking to one knee for the first time in a formal gesture of respect, as Munyiga offered gracious thanks in his careful English. Robbed of words, Beth could only wave and cry, cry and wave, as the car drove away, the Nightingale voices raised as one in a song of farewell.

It was not until she boarded the plane that Beth began to feel unwell, and this she put down to her overtired and emotional state. She slept for much of the journey, waking only to take water before falling back into a restless sleep. The air stewardesses watched the English woman toss and turn in her seat, first rejecting her blanket, then clutching it tightly to her as her temperature rose and fell, and rose again. By the time the plane landed at Heathrow some eight hours later, it was clear that all was not as it should be. Refusing all offers of help, Beth staggered from the plane, her hair lank with sweat, her eyes dull and listless. She had intended to take the shuttle train into London, and from there the Underground to Waterloo, and the train home to Little Bookham. Fortunately for Beth, her mother and Cerys had extracted her flight details from Janet and staked out the arrivals lounge at the airport. The moment she caught sight of her sister, Cerys dashed forward. 'Beth!'

'Don't . . . feel too clever,' Beth mumbled, dropping her bags and collapsing heavily into her sister's embrace. 'Think it's flu.'

'Mum, help me out here, for goodness' sake,' Cerys snapped as Beryl fluttered at her side like a frightened butterfly. 'Take the bags, will you?'

'Oh. Right. Bags, yes,' Beryl dithered, scurrying along behind Cerys, who was half-carrying, half-dragging Beth.

'Just stop here for a second,' Cerys grunted, lowering Beth into the first chair they came to, 'while I get my breath back. Then I'll go and find a wheelchair and we'll get you to the car.'

'I, er, hospital, do you think?' panted Beryl, leaning on the suitcase.

'First things first, Mum. Let's get to the car, and then we'll see what's what.'

'Fine,' Beth moaned. 'Just need to rest.'

Beryl darted forward and peered closely at her daughter for a few seconds. 'Oh!' Then she looked at Cerys, her eyes saucer-wide. 'I think it's malaria.'

'For heaven's sake, mother!' Cerys yelled. 'Now is *not* the time for one of your health rants. Munchausens by proxy, referred hypochondria, whatever you call it. Pack it in, will you?'

'No,' said Beryl, insistently. 'I'm serious. This time I really think it is.'

Chapter Eighteen

'Mum, focus. I need you to focus.'

Cerys looked round to where the ambulancemen were loading Beth's stretcher into the back of the ambulance. 'Mum,' she said, urgently, 'the ambulance is ready to leave. I need to go.' With a muttered oath she forcibly removed her mother's hand from her face. 'Stop with the yoga nose breathing for a minute, alright? Calm down. Here are the keys.' She dangled them in front of her mother's face like a hypnotist's watch. 'Take the car. Call Jenny and Nathan on the number I gave you and tell them what's happened. They'll keep Phoebe as long as necessary, OK?'

'OK,' whimpered Beryl.

'Drive home,' Cerys continued, wishing she had time to write all this down. 'Wait to hear from me, and you can join us when I know where they're going to take Beth.'

'Well, the Hospital for Tropical Diseases, surely,' Beryl stammered.

'Mum, *I don't know*,' groaned Cerys, starting to panic herself as the ambulance revved its engine and the paramedic beckoned to her, his hand ready to close the door. 'I'll call you as soon as I can, OK?' She ran a few steps towards the ambulance, stopped, swore, ran back and pressed a kiss on her mother's forehead. 'It will be OK,' she promised, and charged off again.

'Right,' said Beryl, faintly. 'OK.' She stood there for several seconds, the keys dangling from her hand. 'I wonder where we left the car?' Putting this rather crucial detail aside for the time being, she fished her mobile phone from her handbag and dialled the number Cerys had scrawled painfully onto the back of her hand with one of Phoebe's felt-tips.

In the ambulance, Cerys clutched at the paramedic's arm as they lurched round a corner at speed. 'Sorry,' she said, automatically.

'Don't worry, love,' he replied. 'But you might want to buckle up. We'll try to make up as much time as we can before we hit the London traffic, you see.'

'Right, yes,' gasped Cerys. 'I hadn't thought of that. Tell him to put his foot down.' She fell into a seat and strapped herself in.

'Don't worry,' the paramedic repeated, bracing himself with a well-practised arm as they swung out to overtake a car. 'We'll get there. Your sister's doing OK. My name's Jimmy, by the way.'

'Cerys.' She leaned forward in her seat, watching for the slightest flicker of movement in her sister's face. 'Is she really going to be OK?' She turned her scrutiny on the paramedic, trying to decide whether he was telling the truth or obliged to say something positive in case Beth could hear him.

The paramedic gave her arm a reassuring pat. 'We've made her comfortable,' he said. 'You'll know more when the doctors get a look at her.' He added kindly, 'Why don't you have another look through her bag, see if there's any medication she was taking, anything you might have missed?'

'I've already looked.'

'No harm in double-checking, just to be sure,' he said, calmly. Cerys grabbed Beth's hand luggage holdall, began raking through it, then stopped and forced herself to do a slow, thorough check. This time it yielded results. 'Here!'

'Well done,' said Jimmy, holding out his hand for the box of pills. 'Right. Chloroquine. So she was definitely in a malaria risk zone.' He frowned, weighing up the possibilities, then reached for the radio that connected them to the driver up front. 'Definitely A and E, UCL,' he said, speaking slowly and clearly.

'What does that mean?' Cerys demanded. 'What's wrong with her?'

Jimmy smiled. 'University College London Hospital,' he said. 'We were heading there anyway, but these confirm the decision.' He glanced at the small box in his palm. 'The Hospital for Tropical Diseases is just round the corner from there. Best to let the A and E doctors there take a look at her first to check out the baby, and then we can whip her straight round to the experts if need be.'

'You think it's malaria, then?'

'Pregnancy lowers the immune system, so there's quite a high chance of it, yes.'

'I can't believe it,' Cerys choked. 'Mum was right.' Her hand closed over the phone in her pocket. 'I just need to let a few people know.'

'Fire away.'

'Nathan!' Jenny yelled, racing to the foot of the stairs. 'Naaathaaaann!' Seeing the children clustered about her, their faces upturned in fear at the sight of a real grown-up having a tantrum, she pulled herself together. 'In here, children,' she said in her calmest voice, herding them into the lounge. 'Let's put a DVD on, shall we, as a treat? How about *Mary Poppins?*'

'Yaaaaayyy!' By the time she'd got them lined up on the sofa, pressed play and hurried out, Nathan was halfway down the stairs, his hair pillow-scuffed from an aborted afternoon nap. 'What? What?' he mumbled, half-slipping down the last three steps, even more gangly and uncoordinated than usual.

'In here,' hissed Jenny, yanking him down the hallway and into the kitchen and shutting the door. 'I've just had a call from Beryl – Cerys's and Beth's mum.' Rapidly she filled him in.

Nathan leaned back against the wall, rubbing his eyes. 'Before we leap into action, let's be sure I've got this right,' he said. 'We're to keep Phoebe here . . .'

'For as long as needed.'

'And Cerys's mum Beryl is . . .'

'Lost in a car park but quite alright, she said,' supplied Jenny. 'Yes.'

'OK,' said Nathan, slowly. 'And Cerys is with Beth, on the way to . . .' he paused expectantly, waiting for Jenny to fill in the blank.

'We don't know yet,' she said. 'Oh, hang on, text message.' She snatched up her phone. 'On the way to the Hospital for Tropical Diseases,' she said. 'Suspected malaria.'

'Where the hell's that?'

'Just off Tottenham Court Road,' said Jenny.

'How do you know that?' he asked in amazement.

'I just do.'

'Right,' said Nathan. 'So there's nothing else we can do for now except look after the children.'

'There is one other thing we can do,' Jenny said.

'Pray?'

'OK, two things,' she said, irritably. 'Pray, and call David.' She raised a hand to forestall Nathan's objection. 'Whatever we think of the situation, he does have a right to know. And if you're not going to ring him, I will.'

Nathan's shoulders sagged. 'No,' he sighed. 'I'll do it. What a mess it all is. If only Beth hadn't gone tearing off like that.'

'I think it had been planned for some time, Nathan,' Jenny said, reasonably. 'And you can understand her wanting to get away from here after the funeral.'

'Yes, but she should have taken malaria tablets.'

'I'm sure she *did* take malaria – tell you what, you make the call, I'll make popcorn for the kids, and we can argue about it afterwards, agreed?'

'Agreed.'

David was playing golf with a couple of business associates at the London Golf Club, bizarrely named since it was located in Kent, when his phone rang at the ninth hole.

'Nathan,' he said, surprised and pleased to hear from him after weeks of silence. 'It's great to hear your voice.'

'Where are you, David?' Nathan said, without preamble.

'Playing golf at the London.'

'Can you get to a car?'

'It's a few minutes walk, but yes.'

'Right, I won't waste time. Make your excuses and start

walking. I'll explain on the way. It's an emergency.' Puzzled and alarmed, David did as he was told. Within five strides he was walking briskly, and by ten it was a flat-out sprint, his golf clubs abandoned behind him as he raced for the car. He was on the A20 in less than five minutes, driving like a mad-man, and doing something he hadn't done in a very, very long time – praying.

In the purpose-built forty-three bed unit of the tropical disease and infection unit, Cerys waited in the corridor outside a private room as a consultant performed some checks on Beth. After what felt like an eternity but was in fact only ten minutes, he emerged and spoke briefly to Cerys, his manner professional and reassuring. Two medical students loitered a few yards away, trying to emulate his confident stance without success. 'No immediate danger,' the consultant assured Cerys. 'She will need extremely careful monitoring and we'll be watching her round the clock,' he added, mindful of the need to articulate the possibility of patient deterioration when advising next of kin. 'But there's no immediate cause for alarm. Both she and the baby are stable for the time being.'

'For the time being?'

'As I said, no immediate cause for alarm. You can go in now. A nurse will be along to check on Mrs Hampton in quarter of an hour.'

'Thank you.' With a polite nod, the consultant walked briskly away, the students fawning at his heels like overgrown white-coated dogs.

Cerys entered the room and ran to the bedside, bending over Beth's body. 'Beth?' she said, softly. 'Can you hear me?'

Beth moaned and tossed in her sleep, her face flushed. Cerys pulled up a chair and sat down. 'I'm sorry I was awful to you,' she said after a while, to fill the silence. 'It was a shock.' There was no response but she carried on, hoping Beth could hear her. 'I suppose it was a shock to you as well,' she admitted. 'I never thought of that at the time.' The silence stretched, waiting for more. 'Sorry,' Cerys said, at last. She wondered how Beth's project had gone in Uganda. There hadn't even been time to ask.

Nurses came and went and Cerys wasn't sure how long she sat there, her gaze switching monotonously between the floor, the wall, and Beth's bed. After an hour or so, she fell asleep and was roughly woken by a nurse shaking her shoulder and speaking urgently in her ear. 'Wake up, please. I need you to wait outside. Wake up.'

'Uh? What . . .' She was aware of several people in the room, an impression of swift movement and of orders snapped out and rapidly obeyed. Then she was out in the corridor, confused, shivering, and horribly conscious that something was very wrong. As she stood there staring blankly at the closed door, her mother appeared at the far end of the corridor with Jenny beside her and Rich's friend David loping behind.

'I offered to drive your mum,' Jenny said by way of greeting.

'What's happening?' asked Beryl, fraught and tearful.

'I . . . I don't know,' Cerys said, helplessly. 'They said she was stable, and I sat with her, and . . . then I fell asleep, and the next thing I knew they were chucking me out.'

'I'll soon find out,' David said curtly, striding to the door and trying to enter. He was immediately rebuffed by a nurse who told him in no uncertain terms to stay out. He fell back, and the anxious group huddled together, truly fearful now.

Finally the door opened, and Beth was wheeled out at high speed by a phalanx of nurses and taken away. 'Beth!' Beryl wailed in horror. The consultant emerged from the room last and, recognizing Cerys, approached her first.

'I'm her mother,' Beryl said, pushing forward.

'Mr Clayton,' he introduced himself, offering his hand and glancing at Cerys. 'We met earlier, I believe.'

'Yes,' said Cerys, faintly. 'What's happened to Beth?'

The consultant cast a questioning look at Jenny and David. 'It's alright,' said Cerys, distractedly. 'Tell us.'

Mr Clayton beckoned the group into the now vacant room.

'Please, doctor,' begged Beryl. 'Will Beth be alright?'

Jenny ran her hands tiredly through her unwashed hair. It was the seventh day of waiting, and her nerves were wound tighter than a bowstring at full draw. When Nathan had got up that morning, he had taken one look at her and declared he would work from home. Jenny had laughed at this, a painful, hollow laugh that scratched her throat and hurt her stomach. 'Work from home?' she croaked. 'Good one.'

With four bubbly children tearing about and one near-suicidal friend camped in the guest room, the idea of having sufficient peace to work, or indeed to form any lucid thought process, was a joke. In truth, Jenny was grateful for Nathan's support, knowing the thin screen of normality she'd been holding up for the children was slowly weakening, shot through with a cobweb of hairline cracks as the strain began to tell. It was mid-morning and they were in the garden, the children bowling about on the lawn with play sacks, hoops and beanbags in an impromptu home sports day. 'That was an inspired idea,' she said to Nathan, smiling up at him as he appeared at her side with a loaded tea tray. 'Any change?'

'None.' Nathan put the tray down on the garden table and lowered himself heavily into a chair. 'I can't get through to him, Jen. He won't eat a thing and he's barely touched the water. He's just lying face down on the bed. Thanks, love,' he said as Jenny poured the tea and cut him a generous wedge of Dundee cake. They broke off to cheer enthusiastically as Abigail and Phoebe reached the wooden slide in their sacks, hopping like jumping beans.

'Well done!' called Nathan. 'Now back the other way!' He turned back to Jenny, and shrugged helplessly. 'David keeps telling me to pray for mercy, pray, pray.' He gave a half-smile. 'Shows how desperate he is. You know, I remember years ago, he talked about God . . . then with what happened with Jonathan . . . I think maybe that shut the door on any religious ideas. Anyway, I promised him we'd pray.'

'We've been praying constantly,' Jenny said, tartly. 'Even if it's only five minutes here and there. But somebody's got to keep things ticking over while David's busy with his sackcloth and ashes routine. Sometimes I'd like to lock myself in a darkened room, but there's never a window in the diary.' She threw the cake knife down in despair. 'Sorry, I'm being mean.' Their hands linked beneath the table. 'I'm so worried, Nathan.'

'No news yet today?'

'The consultant doesn't do his rounds until 2 o'clock,' Jenny said. 'But he never has anything new to say in any case. Cerys says he just parrots out the same lines every day about the rare complications of malaria in pregnancy, and coma being a means for the body to put itself to sleep while it heals.' She shrugged, her fingers plucking fretfully at the leg of her linen trousers. 'Some people stay in comas for years.'

'Don't,' said Nathan, gripping her hand more tightly. 'We can't think like that.'

'I know, but I can't help it.'

'At least we know one thing for sure.'

'What's that?'

'David really loves Beth.'

Upstairs in the guest room, David was in the grip of a suffering more intense than anything he had ever experienced. When Carlotta had died there had been grief, but now he was tasting grief mixed with an enormous sense of guilt. It was a bitter cup. He lay as Nathan had described him, face down on the bed, his body limp and his thoughts feverish. After days without food he was drifting in a haze of muddled consciousness and snatched pockets of sleep. Nathan and Jenny came and went, their hands full of food but their mouths empty of the news he so desperately wanted to hear. At rock bottom, David had found himself crying out to the God he'd once believed was there, but had dismissed as fantasy after Jonathan died. What else could he do? He was so used to being in control, but this was way beyond him . . . way beyond anyone except the Divine. So now, in his desperation, he was pleading with God to save Beth and their child, stupidly trying to rationalize his pleas: If you're there, do something. God, if you hear me, help. If you made the world, surely you can save two lives. *If you're God, you could do anything. This would be easy for you, virtually nothing. If you're a loving God, you won't let them die.* He had almost convinced himself that he might get God on his side when two thoughts sliced through his hopes, severing them like cut arteries. *This is a God who let his own Son die. And even if God is real, why would he help me after everything I've done?* For once, David had no answers. He took the pocket-sized Bible from the bedside table and started to leaf through the pages, desperately looking for something, *anything* he could use to persuade this unfathomable God to intervene.

'I can't believe I'm doing this,' he muttered, feeling half-dead from fear and hunger. 'I must be mad.' But he carried on just the same. He had nothing to lose.

'Try, Beth. Please try.' Cerys sat slumped beside the hospital bed, her mother snoring in the armchair opposite. Cerys was holding Beth's limp, lifeless hands with both of hers, hoping to feel a flicker of movement, any sign that her sister was still in there, however small. Squeeze fingers, release. Count to ten. Squeeze fingers, release, count to ten. She must have done it a thousand times with no response but still she persisted, one more time, just one more time, and then another. Because you never knew when Beth might respond. But it was Beryl who stirred, not Beth.

'Leave her be,' she snapped, fear and broken rest grinding a sharp edge to her voice. 'You'll cut off her circulation with all that hand-crushing.'

'Go back to sleep, Mum,' Cerys said dully, allowing her fingers to slide briefly away from Beth's. 'Or go and get a coffee from the machine.'

'I don't want a coffee,' said Beryl, crabby and stiff from the uncomfortable doze in the chair.

Cerys bit back an unkind retort. 'Well, how about you go and freshen up a bit?' she suggested, keeping her temper with the dogged, ingrained patience that had become second nature during the last week. Day had blended into night, then back to day, the seconds passing with agonizing slowness like the drip-drop of fluid passing from the suspended saline pouch into Beth's arm.

'I'm fine as I am,' Beryl muttered, glaring at her daughter as though suspecting Cerys of trying to get rid of her so that she could tell Beth a secret. By this point, neither of them was quite sane.

'Fine. Great.' Cerys picked up Beth's hand and resumed the squeezing routine.

'Please stop that!' wailed Beryl. 'It's like nails down a blackboard.'

'No, Mum, I won't,' Cerys replied, hearing her own voice rising despite her best efforts.

'It won't do any good.'

'It might!' The argument escalated, heated comments flying back and forth across the bed. In a decisive move, Beth reclaimed their attention by having a fit, her body jerking and convulsing beneath the covers.

Jenny and Nathan stood at the door to the guest room, tears like liquid apprehension in their eyes.

'Are you going to tell him?' Jenny whispered. 'I don't think I can do it.'

Nathan bit his lip. 'I'm afraid to. He's not exactly stable, is he? What if he takes it badly? He might do something stupid.' The door opened and David stood there, dishevelled and unshaven, his face haggard. He leaned against the doorframe, his strength sapped after a week without food.

'Is it Beth?' he asked. Nathan nodded as Jenny shook her head. David looked from one to the other. 'Which is it? Yes or no?'

'Cerys called,' Nathan said hesitantly. 'Beth has come round, and she's OK.'

'And the baby?'

'He . . . he didn't make it,' Nathan said, his voice breaking. 'She had a boy, David. It was too soon; they couldn't save him. I'm so sorry.'

Jenny stepped forwards and put her arms round David, crying silently. He accepted the embrace, hanging limply in her arms for a moment. Then he pushed her gently away and stood tall. 'Can you get me a towel, Jen?' he said, evenly. 'I'd like a shower and then something to eat, if you don't mind. Then I'll go to the hospital.'

'I'll drive you,' Nathan offered.

'Thank you.' They watched him nervously as he padded along the landing to the bathroom, waiting for an outburst of emotion that never came.

'He's in shock,' suggested Jenny.

'No,' said Nathan thoughtfully, noticing the small Bible lying open on the bed. 'I don't think he is.'

'I don't know what to make of it. A week spent starving himself half to death, and now he's cool as a cucumber,' she fretted. 'Just like that. Keep an eye on him, Nathan.'

'Don't worry,' said Nathan, seeing his own mystified expression reflected in Jenny's eyes. 'I will.'

Chapter Nineteen

Beth lay in bed, still and silent as a corpse. She was in her old bedroom at her mother's house. They had dragged the bed into the bay window so that she could see outside as she convalesced, watch the world go by. Not that anything did go by in the sleepy back garden, and not that Beth would have paid any attention if it had. She felt removed from the world, as though her soul had tried to follow her baby and not yet come back, but was hovering nearby as if unsure whether the return journey into the empty shell that used to be Beth Hampton was worth it. Perhaps it would be better to give up and travel onwards. After all, what was there to live for here?

Dimly she was aware of the door creaking behind her, and footsteps shuffling across the carpet. Over the past weeks, Beth had learned to identify her main visitors by ear. Shuffling meant it was her mother. Cerys always banged the front door on arrival, although it had long been cured of its former stiffness from the years when they called this place home. Jenny's footsteps were light and swift, always hurrying, Nathan's a calm, measured tread pressing into the floor. Only Phoebe moved on silent feet, flitting to and fro like a fairy. Hers was the only presence Beth could endure for any length of time, because Phoebe didn't bother her with meaningless chat, but climbed without fuss into the bed and snuggled up for a nap beside her aunt, or sat on the window ledge, swinging her legs as she watched the birds fight over worms and scraps of bread. Hunching the covers higher over her shoulders, Beth wished Phoebe were here now instead of her mother.

'Darling, are you awake?' Beryl leaned over the bed, her breath smelling of mint imperials and beneath it, the guilty whiff of tobacco. She must be really worried if she'd taken up smoking again after all these years.

'I don't want to see anyone,' Beth said, stubbornly.

'Your . . . friend is here again,' Beryl said, hopefully. 'Can I send him up?'

'No.'

He came anyway, of course, this time bringing a clutch of flowers, artfully arranged in a cellophane cocoon. He didn't kiss her, having learned better than to try, but lifted her old tub chair over to the bed and folded his long limbs into it.

'I've brought you some flowers,' he said. Beth rolled onto her side, presenting him with her back.

'How are you feeling today?'

She stared at the ceiling and crossed her arms beneath the duvet.

'Your mother hopes you might get up for a while today, perhaps sit out in the garden like you did with Jenny yesterday?' he tried again. 'I could help you, if you'd let me. You might feel better for a bit of fresh air.'

'No, thanks,' she said tonelessly, wondering how long it would be today before he gave up mumbling meaningless platitudes and went away. Half an hour was the current record. Today, however, was different.

'I've had enough of this,' he said, the conversational tone not quite enough to mask the steel in his voice.

'Really? How interesting,' Beth said. 'Why don't you go away, then?'

'Because I love you,' David said, forcefully. 'And it's time for you to be well.' He grasped her by the shoulder and pulled her onto her back. 'Stop being so rude, and look me in the eye when I'm talking to you for a change.'

Beth gaped at him. Weeks of alternate crying, pleading and cajoling had yielded no results and now, with Beryl's permission, David wheeled out the big guns.

'Every time I come here,' he said, glaring down at her, 'I find your mother sitting downstairs weeping with worry. Your sister has been driving up from Brighton every evening to see you, even when you're asleep. Shortly, I expect they'll both have nervous breakdowns from worrying about what's going to become of you. Meanwhile, you lie up here doing your dying swan act, barely eating enough to feed a sparrow, and behaving like a spoiled child.' He paused, watching with interest as the first colour for weeks crept over Beth's face. 'It's not good enough, Beth,' he continued as her pale cheeks darkened to angry red. 'Either curl up and die, or get up and live. Either way, make up your mind and stop being so self-ish, because you're hurting the people who love you most.' In an instant, Beth was bolt upright in bed, flinging the covers off and squaring up to him in her pyjamas.

'How dare you speak to me like that?' she screamed in his face. 'How *dare* you? My husband was murdered!' She launched a flurry of useless punches at his chest. David stood firm and took it without a sound 'My baby died!' Beth cried.

'And I deserved it, and it's all my fault!' She burst into heaving sobs and collapsed on the bed, hiding her face. David sat down in the chair and waited, his face impassive. After a long time, Beth's sobs grew less. Twisting round, she eyed him through a mass of tangled, matted hair. 'Why are you still here?' she sniffed. 'Get out.'

'No,' said David, tenderly. 'Because I loved Rich, and I loved our baby, and I love you. What we did . . .' he stopped, his gut twisting as it would for the rest of his life at the thought of what he'd done to his friend. 'It was wrong, and my wrong was much, much greater than yours, Beth. Believe me.' It was the closest he could bring himself to a confession.

'Then why aren't you having a nervous breakdown, too?'

'Because it won't bring them back,' he said, bluntly. 'And starving myself to death won't make amends.'

Beth thought about this. 'You didn't eat for a week when I was in hospital,' she accused him. 'Jenny told me.'

'Jenny's right,' David replied, 'but don't you see the difference, Beth? Both your lives were hanging by a thread. While there was the smallest chance that you might pull through, I put everything I had into begging God to save you so that I could make amends. I learned so much; you have to believe me, there is nothing beyond his forgiveness.'

'*Forgiveness?* Forgiveness for what we've done? All swept under the carpet as if it never happened?' Beth stared at him, unable to decide whether he was heartless or plain misguided. What kind of screwball theology was this? David returned the stare, his eyes clear and full of purpose.

'When I was fasting, it all became so clear. That's what this is all about. It's insane – but we can both be forgiven.

Forgiven as if it had never happened – that's what I read – anything – anything at all. Because of the man on the cross, Beth, the man who was God and who died for our sin . . . One day, we'll go to where they are, Rich and the baby,' he said, softly. 'And when we do, all things will be made clear and each of us will be called to give an account of our days. Part of me isn't looking forward to that, but I can use the time I have left to make good with my life, and trust – and trust the words I've read are true.' He leaned forward and kissed Beth softly on the brow. She flinched and pulled away from his touch. 'I'll go now. I know you won't believe me, but I'm different. This has changed me,' David said, hoping she would understand.

'Good!' she grunted, confused and not a little frightened.

'One last thing,' David said, lifting the flowers from the floor and propping them on the chair. 'I know what it is to be left behind, Beth. I've lost my wife and my best friend, and now Rich and the baby are gone too.' For a moment he seemed lost, like a small boy far from home. 'For the first time in my life I've realized that what I have done has affected so many people. I have a chance to put that right. I never knew I could, then everything suddenly made sense. I have hope, Beth . . . we have hope . . . to be alive means to hope.'

'Then I'm not really alive,' she said, turning her back on him. She heard the door open, David's parting words all but lost as he left the room.

'I loved them all, and I love you. Come back to me, Beth.'

She threw herself angrily back into bed, scrabbling at the covers and trying to blot out the honesty in those clear eyes, but David's words had got under her skin.

Then suddenly, she remembered with clarity that cross in Uganda, and her 'prayer' to a God she didn't really believe was there. She shut her eyes. What had David said? 'The man who was God and who died for our sin' . . . *Her* sin? Maybe. Forgiveness . . . restoration. Was it possible? And the first sliver of hope began to creep into Beth's heart.

When Beryl knocked timidly at the door later that day, she found her daughter sitting up in bed, pale and troubled but asking for food. Skidding down the stairs so fast she nearly broke her neck, Beryl ran to the phone and breathlessly informed Cerys that the worst was over. 'I don't know what he said, that gentleman friend,' she puffed. 'There was a lot of shouting. Whatever it was, it's rattled Beth's bars and put a bit of fire back in her.' Cerys, who knew more thanks to the ever-tactful intervention of Jenny and Nathan, said less.

'Thank God for that.'

It was as if the words of that day changed her. Beth recovered her strength by slow, steady degrees. This was due partly to the tireless and often suffocating care of her family, but mainly her own decision to 'Get up, get well and get on,' as she put it. Phoebe liked the phrase so much she made it into a song, jigging around Beth's bedroom on tireless feet as she chanted the new motto. One thing about her recovery stood out in sharp relief against the backdrop of support from friends and family. She shunned all contact with David and refused to have his name mentioned in her hearing. He, in turn, appeared to vanish from sight, keeping a low profile socially and putting in long hours at the office. Within two months, Beth was walking into the day clinic at the Hospital for tropical diseases for her final discharge. That night, a celebratory meal was held at her cottage in Little Bookham for a select group of friends.

'So,' said Cerys, raising her glass of champagne aloft. 'A toast, to your good health.'

'Your good health,' chorused the guests, laughing as Beth rolled her eyes, embarrassed by the attention. Jenny scooted along the settee with a plate of profiteroles and winked at Beth. 'You still need a bit of feeding up, in my opinion,' she said. 'Get a couple of these down you.'

'Don't mind if I do,' grinned Beth. They munched in amicable silence, content with the buzz of conversation from the people around them.

'Bet you're glad to be home,' Jenny remarked after a while, using the edge of her sleeve to wipe cream from the corner of her mouth.

'Well, I am,' Beth said. 'But I'm not going to be here for long.'

'What are you talking about?' Jenny was suddenly all rapt attention. Beth grinned at her, then stood up, chinking a knife loudly against her champagne glass.

'I have an announcement to make,' she said, deciding it was better to make it once publicly than go through it ten times in private. Seeing all eyes on her, she almost lost her nerve.

'Spit it out, then,' said Cerys, impatiently. 'Don't keep us in suspense.'

'OK, here goes.' Beth took a deep breath. 'I once heard a famous quote – when you feel as bad as you think it's possible to feel, you should go and do something to help people less fortunate than yourself. Ghandi or Mother Teresa, Janet reckons. Anyway, whoever said it, I agree with them.' She scanned their faces, wondering where the penny would drop first.

'What's your point?' frowned Nathan. 'I'm completely lost already.'

'Lay off the champagne, then,' Jenny said out of the side of her mouth, sending a ripple of laughter through the guests. Beth laughed with them, part of her already missing the comfort of her loyal friends.

'I've decided to go back to Uganda,' she announced. The collective intake of breath sucked at least half the oxygen from the room. 'I'm going back to Lira to teach at the Nightingale school.' She paused, and then thought, what the hell, I've told them this much. 'For a year.' There was a small tinkling sound as a champagne flute was dropped, followed by the hefty thump of Beryl fainting onto the carpet. There was an immediate burst of activity as people rushed around, seeking smelling salts, water, a pillow.

Under cover of the commotion, Cerys looked down at her mother, then up at her sister, who stood alone in the centre of the room, wearing an expression that was half-defiance, half-apology. 'She'll get over it,' she said, cheerfully. 'Try not to get malaria this time, will you?'

'Thanks, Cerys,' Beth said, softly. 'I knew you'd under-stand.'

At the end of the evening, Nathan approached Beth in the kitchen on the pretext of helping with the washing-up.

'What?' she asked suspiciously, as he flourished a tea towel inexpertly.

'Thought you might need a hand in here,' he said, looking wounded.

'And what else?'

'OK, you got me.' He waved the tea towel like a flag of surrender and stepped in close, lowering his voice. 'I wanted to ask whether or not I have your permission to pass on your address, should – anyone – ask for it.'

Instantly Beth's face closed, but her reply was flippant.

'You can give it to anyone who asks,' she said offhandedly. 'It's all the same to me.' Watching Beth's clumsy movements as she fumbled with the plates in the sink, a tiny muscle jumping in her cheek, Nathan thought this wasn't quite true, but he held his peace.

When Beth stepped through the doors of Nightingale school, she turned and looked up at the simple wooden cross that still hung in its place on the wall. 'Well,' she announced. 'I'm back. What do you think of that?' And she smiled.

Once she had set down her cases, she discovered three things in her room. The first was a handwritten invitation from Masani Catherine to join the women for bead making that evening, the writing wobbly, as if the writers had been laughing as she penned the note. The second was a vibrant flowering plant placed on the window ledge by Abbo Maria as she had prepared the room for Beth. The third thing, placed almost as an afterthought on the red blanket that served as a bedspread, was a letter from David Samuel. Beth read it and threw it away. She threw the second letter away as well, and the third and fourth ones. Still, they continued to arrive twice a month. After a while, Beth began to keep them in a tatty cardboard box under her bed, and sometimes she read them again. Eventually, perhaps inevitably, she replied. Just one or two short notes, scribbled almost carelessly during lunchtimes or play times on whatever paper came to hand.

When the year had passed, and she stepped off the plane onto English soil, David was there, waiting. He looked older, and somehow softer, more mellow; but the smile was still charismatic. His face lit up as he saw her, and Beth felt her heart leap.

'Beth!'

'Hi, David.' She looked him up and down, pretending to take stock. 'Still hopeful, I see.'

'Always.'

Smiling, Beth reached out and took his hand.

LIPSTICK CONFESSIONS

Rosie: Note to Self

*Claire Connor with
G.P. Taylor*

Rosie: Note to Self is an uplifting romantic comedy with the themes of loyalty, courage and compassion, set in New York, Oxfordshire and Northumberland. This is the first in the Lipstick Confessions series of novels written by Claire Connor (now Wright) and G.P. Taylor.

She didn't see the man standing staring at his map, and so she butted him right in the back. She rebounded and toppled onto the sidewalk. The coffee cup crunched beneath her and she felt scalding liquid seep through her fingers.

'Don't you look where you're going?' she shouted as someone grabbed her arm from behind and hoisted her to her knees.

'Are you all right?' asked a concerned voice in a warm and unmistakably English accent. Rosie scrambled up and found herself face to face with a faded corduroy jacket. She looked down at the brown stain spreading across the front of her dress, then up at the tall, scruffy guy, whose brown eyes were fixed anxiously on her . . .

978-1-85078-833-1

LIPSTICK CONFESSIONS

The Promise

When Keeping One Means Breaking Another

Claire Connor with G.P. Taylor

The second in the Lipstick Confessions series, *The Promise* follows the story of one man and two women: Sarah who is desperate for a child and free spirit Arima, who belongs to nothing and no one. Or so she thinks . . .

Sarah watched Arima weave across the room, mumbling to herself about keys. This was . . . unbelievable. It couldn't be happening. She seemed sincere but was there a catch?
'Arima. Wait!'
'Yeah?' Arima swayed in the doorway, feeling dead on her feet.
'Promise me you're serious about this. Promise.'
'I promise.'

Can any good come from the promise made between two close friends, Sarah and Arima? Will their friendship endure the trials that follow their life-changing pact? Or will the unforeseen consequences destroy them both?

978-1-85078-885-0

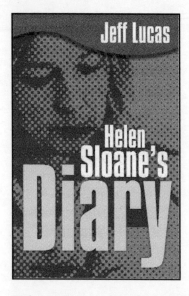

Helen Sloane's Diary

Jeff Lucas

Take Helen, a frustrated 27-year-old rookie social worker. Add Hayley, the world's worst teenager, Kristian, the blond blue-eyed worship leader, faithful friend James, old flame Aaron, corruption, chaos and passion . . . and you've got *Helen Sloane's Diary*.

Blend in a New Age mother, a super-spiritual friend, two deeply unpleasant church members and a personal tragedy, as well as laughter, tears and thought-provoking lines and you have the recipe for a truly great story.

978-1-85078-797-6

Up Close and Personal

What Helen Did Next

Jeff Lucas

Helen Sloane, single and a social worker from Frenton-on-Sea, is struggling to rebuild her life after the murder of her father when she receives a new blow – her beloved church leaders leave. Aaron continually lets her down, James is engaged elsewhere . . . but then she meets a new man, a normal man, a wonderful man.

Has the tide turned for Helen Sloane? Will she learn the identity of her father's killer? Does hard case Hayley join the human race? Is the musical a surprise success or an embarrassing disaster? This is a heart-warming story, full of humour and insight.

978-1-85078-888-1

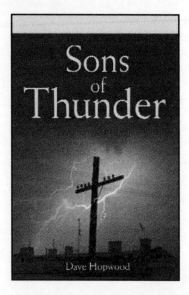

Sons of Thunder

Dave Hopwood

In this poignant and exciting re-telling of the gospel, Dave Hopwood imagines what it would be like if Jesus lived in Cornwall in 2008, hanging around with ordinary guys – guys that don't always get along. How would they react to him, and to each other, when the supernatural starts to take place in front of their eyes? It's going to change them, that's for sure. It's going to change the world . . .

978-1-85078-784-6

The Word of the Wives

Monologues from the unheard women of the Bible

Abby Guinness and Michele Guinness

Behind every great man there's a woman who has to put up with him. Now the unheard women of the Bible speak out in an imaginative collection of monologues, setting the story straight from their unique perspective.

From the amusing to the moving, the arresting to the irreverent, intriguingly charming and alarmingly frank, over twenty-five pieces to read or perform retell the stories of biblical men seen through the discerning eyes of their wives.

978-1-85078-872-0

Authentic

We trust you enjoyed reading this book from
Authentic Media Limited. If you want to be informed
of any new titles from this author and other exciting
releases you can sign up to the Authentic Book
Club online:

www.authenticmedia.co.uk/bookclub

Contact us
By Post: Authentic Media Limited
52 Presley Way
Crownhill
Milton Keynes
MK8 0ES

E-mail: info@authenticmedia.co.uk

Follow us: